STYLE
Michael Jackson

Copyright © 2012 Omnibus Press
(A Division of Music Sales Limited)

Cover designed by Paul Tippett for Vitamin P
Book designed by Paul Tippett and Adrian Andrews for Vitamin P
Picture research by Jacqui Black and Paul Tippett

ISBN: 978.1.84938.819.1
Order No: OP 53933

Exclusive Distributors
Music Sales Limited,
14/15 Berners Street,
London, W1T 3LJ.

Music Sales Corporation,
257 Park Avenue South,
New York, NY 10010, USA.

Macmillan Distribution Services,
56 Parkwest Drive
Derrimut, Vic 3030,
Australia.

Printed in Singapore.

A catalogue record for this book is available from the British Library.

Visit Omnibus Press on the web at www.omnibuspress.com

STYLE

Michael Jackson

STACEY APPEL

OMNIBUS PRESS

CONTENTS

Very few artists have held as big a court around the world as the King of Pop, Michael Jackson.

Along with MJ, there's Elvis Presley, The Beatles and Michael's contemporary, Madonna. These are rock 'n' pop personalities who not only pushed forward the evolution of the recording industry, but also greatly shifted the direction of popular culture. Each of them changed the way we listened to music, how we moved to the groove, what we chose to wear. And when it comes to clothes, Michael's influence as a style icon arguably reaches further than anyone else in entertainment history.

Take for instance heralded fashion heroes Madonna and David Bowie. Madonna may have had her bridal dress and cone bras just as David had his Ziggy Stardust leotards and glitter war paint, but they are both better known for chameleon-like skills that are more aspirational than attainable. The Beatles' *Sgt Pepper* uniforms might be psychedelic classics but pink satin bandleader suits never caught on. And when we think of Elvis, only one image comes to mind: the white jumpsuit.

Compare them all to Michael Jackson, the guy who launched a million red leather jackets. He also had the crystal-studded glove. And the fedora. And the short black trousers, white socks, penny loafers, military jackets. For Michael, these were more than just wardrobe staples or stage costumes. They were part of a uniform that, once established, he remained loyal to for the rest of his career. Every single one of those pieces is so closely associated with him that we often forget they've been around for years. Dress uniforms, for instance, have been around for centuries and were adopted by rock stars in the sixties. These days, you're more likely to hear a teenager refer to these jackets as "Michael Jackson-style" than, say, like those worn by 18th century English officers.

In the seventies, the Jackson 5 represented how the times, they were a changin', sporting a carefully curated and highly marketable image dreamed up by the promotional team at Motown. The appliquéd bell-bottom trousers, immaculately maintained Afro crowns and loud, mixed print get-ups got bolder as the decade shifted forward, an exaggeration of flamboyant African American street fashion. Conversely, it was the littlest J5 brother who, a dozen years later, set the style trends as we all wrapped ourselves in red and black, scrunched up our sleeves, and fruitlessly tried to keep up with him. We also turned our living rooms into makeshift dance studios, spending hours in front of the TV, taping his music videos and learning his equally iconic choreography. *Play--> rewind -->slow --> rewind --> play* went our poor, overworked VCRs.

He often played off the hype, insisting that he wasn't much of a fashion follower but even as a child, he knew the importance of his image. While working the "Chitlin' Circuit" in his pre-Motown years, tiny Michael, all of seven or eight, would stand in the wings and watch his idols, James Brown and Jackie Wilson, perform on stage. Studying every move they made with quiet intensity, he obsessed over their dance moves and the way they held the mic. And also, their shiny shoes and the way they reflected the brightly colored stage lights from above. "My whole dream seemed to centre on having a pair of patent leather shoes," he remembered in his autobiography.

When 'Got To Be There' became a hit in 1972, Michael wanted to perform the song while wearing the applejack hat pictured on the cover of the album. He *knew* the audience would go bananas seeing him in that familiar cap, but his idea was rejected. When Donny Osmond imitated the style and started sporting a similar chapeau, the concert crowds went predictably crazy. Michael knew to always trust his instincts and it was a lesson he never forgot. Later in his career, he almost always wore variations of the white pinstripe suit when performing 'Smooth Criminal' and was never without a red zipper jacket if he was singing 'Beat It'. Even years after these songs disappeared from the charts, the clothes remain inextricably linked to the lyrics and Michael made sure no one forgot them (as if we ever could). He loved his fans like few artists do and pleasing us was of utmost importance. And if sweating beneath a wolf mask during 'Thriller' was going be met with jubilant enthusiasm, then he was all for it. Screams from the audience were like currency to him and in that respect, he was the wealthiest man who ever lived.

He said hello to the WORLD

IMAGE IS EVERYTHING

On August 11, 1969, several hundred lucky guests filed into the Daisy club in Beverly Hills, an exclusive hang-out on Rodeo Drive noted as one of the hippest nightspots in town. Invited by Motown Records' founder Berry Gordy, Jr. and the label's queen songbird Diana Ross, the party-goers — media associates and music industry folk — were promised an evening of cocktails, hors d'oeuvres and fresh new sounds, the latter courtesy of Motown's latest acquisition. "Please join me in welcoming a brilliant musical group," began the invitation, as if Miss Ross had written it herself. "The Jackson 5, featuring sensational eight-year old Michael Jackson, will perform live at the party."

FROM INDIANA TO LA

It had been just over a year since the Jackson 5 signed their record contract when they were unveiled that late-summer evening. Motown, the unstoppable golden child of sixties R&B, suddenly found itself stagnating, with record sales from its once indestructible roster of talent growing soft. When the Jackson 5 first came into Gordy's orbit, he knew they would be the act to bring Motown back to its former chart-topping glory. They were uniquely talented and incredibly driven, not to mention possessed of the kind of photogenic good looks that drive young girls bananas. After the signing, the J5 spent a year working inside Detroit's Hitsville USA studios before Gordy felt they were ready to join him in Los Angeles, Motown's new home. When it was time, he phoned the Gary, Indiana-dwelling family, had them pack their belongings and move 2,000 miles across the country to posh new digs in southern California. Only days later, Michael and his brothers were at the Daisy, entertaining a group of people who would become an important piece in the promotional puzzle of this irresistible new quintet.

> When the Jackson 5 first came into Gordy's orbit, he knew they would be the act to bring Motown back to its former chart-topping glory.

CUTE-AS-A-BUTTON

As their inaugural performance began, the Jackson brothers took to the club's stage and performed a short set of hits from the Motown catalog. Dressed in identical lime green sleeveless suits and floral printed dress shirts (ensembles which mother Katherine Jackson had purchased off-the-rack back in Gary), the boys won over the audience with their confidence, professionalism and stylised dance moves. But just as the invitation had singled him out, it was little Michael who left everyone speechless. He was as pitch perfect as he was cute-as-a-button with an astounding vocal range and emotional depth far beyond his (actual) eleven years. Singer Smokey Robinson described the youngster as "a little old man in a little boy's body" and happily conceded that Michael's rendition of The Miracles' 'Who's Loving You', which Robinson had penned, was the only version that mattered.

DIANA'S DARLINGS

But for Michael, the soiree not only served as a lesson on how to captivate a room full of grown-ups, but also taught him the importance of a carefully crafted image. Motown's publicity department had already set forth the "myth" of the Jackson 5, the one where Diana Ross had "discovered" the group while in Gary, Indiana touring with The Supremes and, so enamoured, presented them to Gordy. Initially, the kids resisted perpetuating such a lie (in actuality, it was singers Gladys Knight and Bobby Taylor who first brought the boys to Motown's attention). But Gordy explained to them the importance of "public relations", which he also used as an excuse for shaving two years off of Michael's age, making him appear even more precocious than he already was.

His brothers may have still been unmoved, but Michael gleefully bought into this new idea called "PR". When journalists asked him how he got started in show business, he would immediately roll out his favourite line with a wink and a smile: "After singing for four years and not becoming a star, I thought I would never be discovered — that is, until Miss Ross came along to save my career."

"I figured out at an early age that if someone said something about me that wasn't true, then it was a lie," he would explain years later. "But if someone said something about my *image* that wasn't true, then it was OK."

> "I figured out at an early age that if someone said something about me that wasn't true, then it was a lie. But if someone said something about my image that wasn't true, then it was OK."

The Jackson 5 often wore these yellow suits before Berry Gordy decided that the boys needed a youthful upgrade.

THEY GOT THE FEELIN'

When the Jackson 5 auditioned for Motown in 1968, squeezed into a Hitsville rehearsal room in front of company executives and a movie camera, they did so by stringing together a handful of rhythm and blues tunes like the Temptations' 'Ain't Too Proud To Beg', 'I Got The Feelin'' by James Brown and 'Tobacco Road', a popular blues standard penned in 1960. Michael, a master showman at the ripe old age of nine, matched the music and singing with spins, splits and "whoops" that would do JB proud. The usually jaded Motown troops were instantly captivated. Even Berry Gordy, who had sworn never to sign another child act after facing problems with Little Stevie Wonder, was won over. However, Gordy had something entirely different in mind when he began developing the Jackson 5 musical style. "My process was not to have Michael do what he was doing," he would explain. "The James Brown-type stuff was way beyond his years." He began grooming Michael to channel a little less JB and more Frankie Lymon, the teenage R&B singer who had a string of hits in the mid-fifties with his group, The Teenagers. A perkier, more jubilant sound was the order, one that showcased Michael's natural "passionate, young kid energy" which he had in spades.

THE CORPORATION

Therefore, in the days following the Jackson 5's winning debut at the Daisy, Gordy assembled a team of songwriters and arrangers for the sole purpose of developing zippy new material for the group. Dubbed the Corporation, this four-man production squad included perennial Motown players Freddie Perren, Deke Richards, Alphonzo Mizell and Berry Gordy himself. The collective quickly knocked out 'I Want You Back', an effervescent jam of puppy love and teenage yearning that in emotion if not in tempo recalled Lymon's 'Why Do Fools Fall In Love?' With its funky bassline, heavy percussion and pass-around vocals shared by Michael and Jermaine, the tune cast the J5 as Gordy's very own little Sly & The Family Stone. 'I Want You Back', which became their debut single, also positioned them as Motown's response to the optimistic "peace and love" ideology that coincided with the cultural changes of the sixties and early seventies.

I WANT YOU BACK

With a hot new single ready to go, the creative forces at Motown focused on the Jackson 5's visual image which was also in need of a youthful update. Shortly after their Daisy debut, the J5 had made their first television appearance on the Miss Black America Pageant. While running through a short set list that included the Isley Brothers' 'It's Your Thing', they sported those same pea green polyester ensembles they had worn before. Two months later when 'I Want You Back' was ready for promotion, those dowdy duds were again resurrected as they performed the song on Diana Ross' television special, *The Hollywood Palace*. By this point, it became clear that it was time to retire the matching suits, a look popularised by older singing groups of the sixties which had become decidedly outmoded by 1969. The boys needed stage threads that were young and groovy and reflected the more individualistic approach to fashion that was indicative of the forthcoming decade. Gordy assigned Suzanne de Passe, then vice president of creative operations at Motown and stylish young thing in her own right, the task of making over the Jacksons from miniature soul men into the most happenin' heartthrobs on the playground scene.

Opposite: Daring colour combos, hippie fringes and punchy patterns became hallmarks of J5 fashion.

THE ED SULLIVAN SHOW

By the time the Jackson 5 performed on *The Ed Sullivan Show* on December 14, 1969, the changes were obvious: out were the head-to-toe identical, slightly ill-fitting ensembles and close cropped hair, very much in were separate looks for each brother, styles that complemented one another but remained distinctive, all topped off with Afro halos. De Passe hit up the vibrant hippie boutiques of New York City's Greenwich Village for much of the show wardrobe, including that memorable purple fedora Michael wore with such aplomb. His entire ensemble — the beaded fringe vest, flared trousers and ankle boots — were typical of psychedelic fashion at the time, a look that, like their sound, hinted at Sly & The Family Stone. De Passe's wardrobe styling fused with Michael's passionate vocals, perfectly executed spins and infectious smile proved to be a winning combination. "The day after the Sullivan show, all hell broke loose in the press," Berry Gordy remembered in his autobiography. "The show was heralded as a phenomenon by everybody."

NUMBER ONE

In a little over a month, 'I Want You Back' shot to number one on the *Billboard* magazine Hot 100 Chart, the American music industry's de facto scale of a song's popularity. After its success, Gordy instructed the Corporation to develop a similar tune, one that continued on with the lively spirit of its predecessor. Motown's main man was determined to see his prediction come true, the one in which he promised the Jackson brothers they'd have three number one songs in a row.

ABC

The ebullient school-yard ditty 'ABC' was swiftly written, recorded and released in February 1970, topping the charts and knocking The Beatles' 'Let It Be' out of the number one position. 'The Love You Save' followed suit three months later, thereby fulfilling Gordy's premonition of a trio of chart-topping singles. But all expectations were surpassed when Motown dropped the Jackson 5's first ballad, 'I'll Be There', which not only joined the previous tunes in reaching the same prime chart position, but had a more successful run than any other song previously released by the label. The J5 also became the first act in recording history to reach the number one spot with their first four singles, selling a phenomenal ten million records by the end of the year.

> "The day after the Sullivan show, all hell broke loose in the press. The show was heralded as a phenomenon by everybody."

Above left: Michael was an ardent fan of Sly & The Family Stone, as was Berry Gordy, who used the rock/funk band as inspiration for the Jackson 5 sound and style.
Above right: When the young brothers made their legendary appearance on *The Ed Sullivan Show*, the Sly Stone influence was apparent.
Right: A trip to the beach for an 'ABC' promotional photo shoot.

WATCH AND LEARN

While the Corporation was busy bulking up the J5 song catalogue, Suzanne de Passe served as a manager and mentor to Michael, Marlon, Jackie, Jermaine, and Tito. They took classes on proper table manners and grammar skills and were taught the *preferred* way to answer questions that might be asked in interviews. Discouraged was engaging in any discourse that could be construed as controversial and endorsing the burgeoning Black Power movement was forbidden. To Gordy, keeping the J5 as amiable as possible was crucial to the group's success, especially as he aimed to break them through to a white audience. (Eventually, Motown prohibited the media from asking any questions about drugs or politics.) However, the boys' ever-growing Afros signalled Black Pride without them ever having to say a word.

Above: Michael is all smiles on the set of
The Jackson 5 Show.
Left: The Jackson 5, performing on the *Diana!*
television special in 1971, decked out in flashy,
Boyd Clopton-designed outfits.

SLIDE-AND-TURN

De Passe also began developing and updating the Jackson 5's signature brand of joyful choreography, beginning with 'I Want You Back' which she and the boys had worked out in her own living room. The J5's initial performance style could best be described as a mini James Brown fronting the Four Tops; Michael in front showing off his improvisational slide-and-turn footwork while the rest of the family stood behind him stepping and swaying in quiet unison. With de Passe in charge that all changed, and getting Michael to stop imitating the Godfather of Soul was her top priority.

Michael, who had grown up worshiping James Brown and Jackie Wilson, had already perfected their dance moves and mannerisms. As a small child, he watched them closely when they appeared on television and became aggravated if the camera zoomed in on their faces, thus preventing him from studying their feet.

WATCHING... LEARNING

When the Jackson 5 started performing on the Chitlin' Circuit, a series of venues which hosted African American entertainers during the age of segregation, they opened for those very same acts Michael used to observe on TV. While his brothers were off eating or chilling out during downtime, Michael stood in the wings of the stage, hiding in the curtains taking in the performances of veterans. "After studying James Brown, I

knew every step, every grunt, every spin and turn," he would recall. But while all that studying paid off in getting Michael and his brothers a Motown contract, de Passe and Gordy both thought it would be better if they had a style that was a little more contemporary. Under de Passe's tutelage, the Jackson 5 performed routines that were high in energy, bouncier and more in line with how young people were dancing at American discotheques.

HYSTERIA

After a smattering of one-off concert dates in Los Angeles, San Francisco and Philadelphia, the Jackson 5's first proper national tour across the United States commenced in late 1970. As their songs sailed up the music charts, the boys were confronted in each city with ever more hysterical herds of screaming fans. Mostly girls and almost entirely underage, they were inescapable, showing up not only at concerts but hotels, department stores and airports, any place that the boys were rumoured to be.

While his older brothers often got a chuckle out of their own version of Beatlemania, Michael understandably wasn't quite as enthused; the scene was tremendously overwhelming for a sensitive adolescent boy. The unruly mob scenes ultimately forced the Jacksons to hole themselves up in hotel rooms, which was one of the reasons why Michael despised being on tour throughout most of his life.

"After studying James Brown, I knew every step, every grunt, every spin and turn."

Above: Even as a child, Michael worked tirelessly to perfect his dance moves (left), many of which were lifted from his idol, James Brown (right).
Opposite: In 1972, Michael wore this mustard yellow suit on multiple occasions, including this appearance on *The Dating Game.*

GOT TO BE THERE

The days in between concert dates were filled with recording sessions for not only the group (three full-length albums were released in 1970 alone) but also solo efforts for Michael, starting with 'Got To Be There', released in 1971. Television bookings became a staple in the Jackson 5 schedule, dropped in amongst tours and records. *The Andy Williams Show, Diana!, The Flip Wilson Show, Soul Train, The Sonny & Cher Comedy Hour, American Bandstand* and *Sesame Street*, appearances often consisted of multiple musical numbers as well as sketch comedy segments, all of which required hours of rehearsal time, making even brief segments incredibly time-consuming. Michael even became a surprise contestant on *The Dating Game*, asking three "delightful damsels" such revealing questions as "What makes you a little bitty pretty one?" while his own interests were noted as "sketching and drawing, playing basketball, candy and bubblegum." Wearing a dandy mustard yellow suit, brown shirt and floral tie, 14-year-old Michael became arguably the most delightful little bachelor in the history of televised matchmaking.

GOIN' BACK TO INDIANA

The J5 became such a big draw that they soon headlined several specials of their own. In 1971, there was *Goin' Back To Indiana* which featured the group in a series of comedic skits connected by performances of the group's biggest hits. Bill Cosby, Tommy Sommers, Rosie Grier, and Diana Ross all took part in the special which was topped off by live concert footage in which those angelic Jackson brothers suddenly transformed into pelvic thrusting showmen who could deliver the funk as well as any seasoned musician twice their age. Performing cover versions of Sly & the Family Stone's 'Stand!' and Isaac Hayes' slow grooving 'Walk On By', they proved not only that they could get *down* but also, a little bit dirty. For *The Jackson 5 Show* (1972), the brothers sang songs and traded quips decked out in a never ending array of orange and yellow colourblock outfits. But while these cheerful programs were not particularly edgy or political, just seeing young black faces on primetime television showed how the J5 were helping to break down the colour barriers of traditional Hollywood broadcasting.

Above left: Diana Ross helped Michael develop an appreciation for the visual arts.
Above right: The Jackson 5 with Bill Cosby, on the set of *Goin' Back To Indiana*.
Opposite top: A rare animation cell from *The Jackson 5ive* cartoon series.

PL-65   F-55   B5

J5 AS CARTOON CHARACTERS

The group became even more ubiquitous once their Saturday morning programme *The Jackson 5ive* debuted in the autumn of 1971. A spirited cartoon series starring two-dimensional likenesses of the talented quintet, *The Jackson 5ive* was produced at Rankin/Bass studios (the company known for stop-motion classics like *Rudolph The Red-Nosed Reindeer*) and directed by Robert Balser, who had previously worked on the Beatles' animation feature *Yellow Submarine*.

When Balser was handed the first batch of scripts, he was horrified by how silly and violent the narratives were. *The Jackson 5ive* was the first cartoon strip centred entirely around a cast of black youths and knowing how important the project was, he was adamant about totally rewriting the episodes to reflect more positively on the Jackson kids. A good deal of attention was paid to the details, especially in regards to how the J5 looked and moved. An artist even spent time in

the recording studio with the group so as to best capture their hand gestures and facial features. "The one thing we didn't want was just white kids washed black," affirmed Jim White, Motown's vice president of production. Due to scheduling conflicts, the Jacksons didn't provide the speaking voices, only the music which was pulled from the records.

Of all the brothers, it was Michael who most adored his caricatured self. "I loved being a cartoon. It was so much fun to get up... to watch cartoons and look forward to seeing ourselves on the screen." An avid fan of animation pioneer Walt Disney, his affection for the art form increased after *The Jackson 5ive* began airing.

Drawing would eventually become one of his most treasured pastimes, a hobby that was ignited by none other than Diana Ross. It was Ross who encouraged Michael to doodle and paint, buying him art supplies and taking him to museums while he briefly lived with her after landing in LA.

SELLING THEIR SOUL

As his young protégés sat comfortably atop the *Billboard* charts and their live appearances were met with the kind of pandemonium only hormonal teenage girls could create, Gordy and company began drafting plans for a marketing blitz to help spread the Jackson 5 love around even further. Inexpensive products emblazoned with J5 imagery like stickers, posters and badges sold so well that toys, book bags and sweatshirts soon hit the market as well. Motown created *TcB!* – Taking Care of Business – magazine, a quarterly fanzine devoted entirely to the lives of the Jackson boys.

An official J5 logo was designed, curly and cartoon-like, with hearts growing out of the letters, sure to please every girl under the age of 15. An endorsement deal was signed with Post cereal in which the group appeared in a series of goofy television ads for the company ('ABC' seemed especially tailor-made for the alphabet-shaped morsels of Post's 'Alpha-Bits'). Their faces were printed on the product packaging, often with a special prize attached to the box, like recordings of their songs which could be cut out and listened to on a real record player. They even had a minor hit with 'The Jackson 5 Rapping', a record that consisted not of music, but of the boys talking about themselves and to each other.

HEART-SHAPED

By this time Suzanne de Passe had handed over wardrobe duties to Boyd Clopton, a designer who also created wild stage garb for the 5th Dimension and the Rolling Stones. Clopton became responsible for keeping the boys looking up-to-date and sprightly while also young and accessible to their adolescent fan base. He dressed the group in customised teeny bop finery, pastel tie dyes, velvets, and mixed prints decorated with fringe, whimsical appliques and heart-shaped accents which matched the J5's logo.

Clopton was also the designer tapped to cook up a Jackson 5 retail fashion line which unfortunately never came to fruition. Fred Rice, the man behind the merchandise bonanza (he had previously worked with the Beatles and the Monkees) told *Creem* magazine in 1971: "This is the first time in my 24 years in the business that we've seen anything like this. They're heroes, it's unbelievable." Similarly, Motown's publicity director Junius Griffin proclaimed, "There's nothing out there like them. They're wholesome, clean, cute, and black."

> **Motown's publicity director Junius Griffin proclaimed, "There's nothing out there like them. They're wholesome, clean, cute, and black."**

Above: From pastel tie-dye to heart motifs and playful colour-blocking, Boyd Clopton's costumes for the J5 were geared to make the teeny boppers lose their minds.
Opposite: A series of on-the-road snapshots taken by photographer Barry Plumber, during the J5's visit to Europe in 1972.

BUBBLEGUM SOUL SALVATION

One of the reasons the Jackson 5's popularity was so frenzied from the get-go was due to a drought of young, black singers that might appeal to the subteen set. In fact, it was a musical demographic that had yet to be properly filled. "The typical black star is not a skinny, hairy rocker in a T-shirt," observed *Life* magazine in 1970. "He's a middle-aged soul man like James Brown, a matronly gospel lady like Aretha Franklin or a glamorous Persian Room chanteuse like Diana Ross or Dionne Warwick."

Simply put, black youths may have been listening to these artists but they couldn't necessarily relate to them in the same way the young girls did back in 1964 when they were stricken with Beatlemania. Enter the Jackson 5: a group of good-looking, close-knit African American brothers who possessed smooth vocals, dressed in fab frippery and kicked out the jams with some slick dance moves. And with all five boys

landing between the ages of 11 and 18, there was sure to be at least one favourite brother for every middle and high school girl to swoon over. Motown even created separate "personalities" for each of the boys: Jackie was the athlete, Jermaine was the dream boat, applejack cap-wearing Tito was interested in photography and mechanics, while Marlon was a jokester who loved to dance. Michael was the energetic frontman, overflowing with talent but with cheeks that were just begging to be squeezed.

Opposite: Western-style applique and embroidery was a signature design element of International Costume Company.
Above: Boldly attired in red and yellow, the Jackson 5 perform on the classic British television programme *Top Of The Pops* in 1972.

> Michael was the energetic frontman, overflowing with talent but with cheeks that were just begging to be squeezed.

THE FIRST BLACK BUBBLEGUM HEROES

With the Jackson 5 quickly turning into one the hottest properties on Top 40 radio, they not only became heroes for young black Americans but they also revived a bubblegum pop scene that had been largely neglected since the Beatles grew out their mop tops and sprouted facial hair.

The Osmond Brothers — familiar song-and-dance television personalities with a penchant for barbershop harmonies — switched gears and released 'One Bad Apple', a poppy, soul-tinged tune sung by the youngest brother, Donny. It was so similar in sound to the J5 that Jackson relatives thought it *was* a J5 track (in referencing the Osmonds, *Life* magazine commented "you'd swear at times you were watching the Jackson Five in white face"). The Partridge Family, a TV sitcom about a musical family band, began airing in the fall of 1970 with a cast that included the perfectly coiffed David Cassidy. Next onto the bandwagon were the Sylvers who, like the Osmonds, sounded very similar to the J5 but had more limited success. The Canadian co-ed De Franco Family joined the party and came equipped with 13-year-old falsetto-voiced Tony, whose fringe haircut and studded denim play clothes made him a natural player in the race for preteen pin-up supremacy. Even the non-singing, non-dancing Brady Bunch siblings started making (bad) music while attempting (really bad) choreography.

PIN-UPS

With this dreamy new facet of young Hollywood begging for coverage, the seventies became a boom time for the teenage magazine industry thanks in large part to the pioneering Jackson 5. But despite their massive record sales, the attendance at their concerts, the fainting tween girls, Michael, Jermaine and Jackie always landed on far fewer pages and covers than David, Donny and Tony. Seemingly cut from the same cloth, feather-headed lads in tight tees and hipster trousers populated a paper landscape that lacked any real diversity. But while *Tiger Beat* and *16* magazines were embarrassingly short-sighted, *Right On!* more than made up for when it commenced publication in 1971. Similar to its competition in design and layout but instead aimed at a young "urban" readership, *Right On!* featured at least one Jackson brother on every cover for over three years running. African-American music and culture critic Nelson George described *Right On!* as "the *Tiger Beat* of the bushy Afro, bell-bottomed, body poppin' *Soul Train*-watching generation".

Above: Again wearing Boyd Clopton, but this time in mix-match prints of black and white.
Opposite: Once the Jackson 5 hit it big, other family acts, like the Sylvers, the Osmonds and the DeFranco Family, started populating the music charts.

The Jackson 5 had blossomed into such a hot commodity that they became unwitting trendsetters in the recording industry, inspiring other musical acts to try and cop their style. The most notable offender was the Osmonds, another quintet of five brothers with a younger sixth held in reserve.

They had become likable fixtures on American television throughout the sixties, and had a knack for harmonious barbershop-style tunes and were as wholesome as they were pitch-perfect. However, after the Jackson 5's popularity skyrocketed in 1970, the Osmonds' management jumped on the opportunity to turn their kids into equally prominent teeny bop idols.

They even had their answer to Michael in shaggy-headed Donny who, at age 12, was also very close in age to the youngest Jackson.

At the end of 1970, the Osmond Brothers released 'One Bad Apple' which became as big a smash as any of the J5's previous hits. At first, many listeners thought it was a J5 song with its comparably bouncy yet soulful melody and high-pitch lead vocals. In fact, 'One Bad Apple' was written with the Jackson 5 in mind but when it was presented to Berry Gordy, Jr., he turned it down. Often referred to in the press as the Jacksons' "white counterparts", the Osmonds even adopted a Jackson-esque wardrobe of fringe-trim vests and kaleidoscopic prints which looked slightly less superfly on a bunch of living, breathing Ken dolls.

Despite the fact that the Osmonds landed many more teen magazine covers in their prime, they were initially regarded as the inferior knock-offs of the *Tiger Beat* scene. "Leave it to the whites to always have to follow," proclaimed comedian Richard Pryor, a sentiment which was shared by many.

In the end, peace was restored to the bubblegum playground when it became clear that the pop world was big enough for both groups to peacefully co-exist; the Jacksons stuck to the winning formula they created while the Osmonds found a sound and fan base all their own.

Luckily, the families never admitted to feeling any competition between each other; they seemed to leave that up to their managers. However, the groups continued to have parallel careers throughout much of the seventies.

The ballad 'Ben' was first recorded by Donny. However, the ever crafty Berry Gordy Jr was able to snag the tune for Michael. In Michael's hands, 'Ben' won a Golden Globe award and was nominated for an Oscar in 1972.

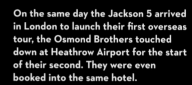

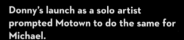

On the same day the Jackson 5 arrived in London to launch their first overseas tour, the Osmond Brothers touched down at Heathrow Airport for the start of their second. They were even booked into the same hotel.

Donny's launch as a solo artist prompted Motown to do the same for Michael.

A year after the first episode of the *Jackson 5ive* Saturday cartoon premiered in 1971, *The Osmonds* began airing, which was also a weekly animated series. Both shows were created by Rankin-Bass studios.

In January 1976, Donny Osmond and sister Marie premiered the aptly named *Donny & Marie* show on ABC. That summer, CBS aired *The Jacksons*, a similar song-and-dance-and-act programme starring not only the Jackson brothers, but all three sisters.

In 1974, both the Osmond Brothers and the Jacksons began extended engagements in Las Vegas (at the Tropicana and MGM Grand, respectively) performing a string of shows that combined music and acting, extravagant costumes, and flashy stage sets.

In the early 2000s, Donny and Michael were discussing working on a duet together, a cover of Stevie Wonder's 'I Wish'. Unfortunately, Michael had to pull out of the project to focus on clearing his name in his upcoming court trial.

GEARED TO BLOW YOUR MIND

It has been said that the "shelf life" of the average teen idol is about two years and by that criterion, the Jackson 5 were well passed their expiration date when their record sales finally began to dip. In 1973, *Skywriter* and *G.I.T.: Get It Together*, as well as Michael's *Music & Me* all missed the mark chart-wise. Attempts to bring the brothers to the big screen also failed. An ill-fated documentary called *The Jackson 5 in Africa*, about the boys' six-day tour of Senegal in 1974, never saw a wide theatrical release. Likewise, a film called *Isomen Cross And Sons* which cast the family as slaves during the mid 19th-century never even entered production. Motown was getting impatient and all but wrote the group off. However, the Jackson brothers did have one more showstopper waiting in their funky arsenal. It was called 'Dancing Machine' and it was *epic*.

DANCING MACHINE

The final track on *G.I.T.*, 'Dancing Machine' was as slick as it was funky, a disco-flavoured floor-stomper that was void of the sugar-pop sweetener sprinkled over their early hits (Michael later referred to the song as "our rite of passage into the adult world"). It also showcased the new, slightly deeper singing voice of the now 15-year-old frontman. The first televised performance of 'Dancing Machine' was on *Soul Train*, the syndicated Saturday morning dance show that was a weekly must-watch event for young, hip black kids across America.

THE ROBOT

Still sporting impeccably maintained Afros, the group appeared in more subdued attire than in the past: white platform boots with coordinated bell-bottom and top ensembles splashed with rhinestones. It was during this performance that Michael, in baby blue sweater vest and white trousers, debuted his version of a mechanical freestyle dance routine that was already popular in urban nightclubs. Called The Robot, the dance combines syncopated lock-and-release gestures with popping and mime. Many *Soul Train* dancers were already incorporating robotic moves into their choreography prior to Michael's performance and most were tickled that he adopted The Robot and made it his own. The jerky movements of the dance were the perfect accompaniment to a track about a hottie who was "built with space-age design".

The song's release couldn't have been timed more perfectly: 'Dancing Machine' landed just as disco fever took off and was played non-stop in the dance clubs that were springing up across the world. The tune went viral and led to a string of television spots in which Michael's robotic routine became more elaborate with each performance, leaving the audience increasingly spellbound. On *The Merv Griffin Show*, he even broke away from the stage, running into the audience, encouraging them to sing along with him. He seemed so poised and at ease in that sea of strangers that it is very hard to believe how young he still was. It was quite another story offstage, where Michael was a sweet but gawky teenager, incredibly shy and in the midst of a growth spurt (literally and artistically).

Fuelled by Michael's mesmerising interpretation of The Robot, 'Dancing Machine' popped-and-locked all the way to number two on *Billboard*'s Hot 100 and number one on the Hot Soul Singles chart. It was such a dazzling success that in late 1974, Motown built another LP around the single. *Dancing Machine* the album was Motown's thinly veiled attempt to squeeze every last penny out of what was to become the J5's last hit for the label. But for Michael, the song's success became a lesson about the power of visuals and how the song's rise up the charts was directly related to his performances on television.

Opposite: By the mid-Seventies, the J5 were wearing more suits, usually highly embellished numbers from International Costume Company.

Clockwise from top left: An illustration by Pete Menefee, a prolific Hollywood costume designer who worked on *Goin' Back To Indiana*; Michael dancing with Cher on her eponymous TV show in 1975; wearing more International Costume Company ensembles, the group performs on *The Bob Hope Show* in 1973.

WHAT HAPPENED IN VEGAS

In early 1974 after returning from an Africa pilgrimage, Papa Joe announced to his children that they were headed to Las Vegas. The news was met with an almost universal groan from the Jackson kids. Vegas, with its miles of casinos, velvet curtain showrooms and schmaltzy lounge lizards, had lost much of the lustre that had shone during the Rat Pack's reign of the fifties and sixties. Less than thrilled with the arrangement, Michael's brothers pictured Sin City as a town where has-been entertainers played when the hits dried up.

Michael, however, was enthusiastic. He viewed Las Vegas as an essential element in the show business institution, a town that Sammy Davis, Jr. (whom he greatly admired) helped to integrate by refusing to perform at venues that practised racial segregation. Michael wanted to be a part of that tradition and welcomed the engagement with open arms. However, the higher powers at Motown objected and refused to get involved, reportedly telling Joe, "If you decide to do this thing, you're doing it on your own."

RANDY, JANET & LATOYA JOIN UP

So without their label's assistance or blessing, the Jackson family commenced a two-week residency of their new theatrical extravaganza at the MGM Grand in April 1974. Prompted by the Osmond family who had added the youngest siblings to their own successful Las Vegas show, the ever competitive Joseph incorporated Randy, Janet and the marginally talented LaToya into the family act. Backed by a large orchestra, the troupe plunged into a set list that included their biggest smashes interspersed with covers of other pop songs, comedy routines and jokey impersonations of everyone from the Andrews Sisters to the Supremes.

Janet and Randy were often credited with stealing the show, performing gut-busting impressions of Sonny & Cher and Mickey & Sylvia (Vegas is also where Janet honed her famous Mae West routine decked out in miniature sequined gown and feather boa). So successful was the show that after the initial run, it returned to Vegas for several more engagements.

The revue featured all the flashy accoutrements that were typical of a seventies Vegas showcase, including gaudy sets, fireworks and embellished polyester tuxedos, the latter designed by Ruth West of the International Costume Company. A veteran of the fashion industry who also outfitted Ann-Margaret, the Miracles and Pam Grier in the film *Foxy Brown*, West joined the Jackson 5 creative team back in 1972 and eventually went on to replace Boyd Clopton as their chief costumer. She was noted for spending time with her clients watching them perform to better customise looks for their specific needs which came in handy; when Michael had gotten into the expensive habit of throwing his jackets into the audience, West started whipping up scarves for him to toss instead.

For the Las Vegas show, and most of their public performances, West dressed them in matching suits which, after years of individualised looks, had become trendy again for young black artists, an affectionate throwback to soul groups of the sixties. West's two- and three-piece cuts were always kitted out with razzle-dazzle details like serpentine sequins, floral embroidery and western wear motifs. She is also the first person to outfit Michael in garments bedecked with crystal studding, a detail that would eventually become his trademark.

Opposite: When Jermaine left the group in 1975, Randy replaced him as the official 5th member.
Above: Snapshots from the road in 1974 and 1975.

KEEP ON DANCING

Legendary hoofer Fred Astaire once told Michael Jackson, "I didn't want to leave this world without knowing who my descendant was. Thank you." Michael was certainly one of the last, great song-and-dance men to grace the stage and screen, someone who is as highly regarded for his rhythmic virtuosity as he was for his recordings, and sometimes more so. In fact, he is one of the only performers whose dance moves are as recognisable and imitated as his music and clothing. And he knew this all too well, which is one of the reasons why he rarely changed up the choreography that was so closely associated with each hit song.

For instance, just as he would always wear a red zipper jacket while performing 'Beat It' in concert, he would also re-create the signature gangland line dance and mock knife fight. Even when running through his tried-and-true Jackson 5 medley, he would rock out the same Motown routines he performed with his brothers in the seventies knowing how his fans would scream when they recognized the steps.

In 1983, he changed the way music videos looked when he introduced intricate moves and ensemble dancing into promotional videos; today, it's almost unheard of not to have a Top 40 singer backed by an able dance squad. His choreo has been re-created on the big screen (13 Going On 30), the computer screen (YouTube's orange-clad Filipino inmates video) and in three-dimensional real life (the annual simultaneous, worldwide dance-off, Thrill The World).

A perfectionist to a fault, one of his most trusted choreographers, Vincent Paterson, would often describe how Michael would "work on one step for hours at a time until he was so comfortable with it he never had to think about it again". In August of 2010 he was given one of the highest honors a dancer can receive when he was inducted into the C.V. Whitney Dance Hall of Fame at the National Museum of Dance in Saratoga Springs, New York. Joining an elite club that includes Astaire, Martha Graham and Bill "Bojangles" Robinson, Michael is the only pop star to have been given such an honor. Now the only question is, if Michael is descended from Fred Astaire, who is descended from Michael?

The Anti-Gravity Lean
Achieved through invisible wires and camera editing, the "lean" from 'Smooth Criminal' was so magical and epically cool that even the Tin Man from Oz would have been impressed. Michael replicated it in concert with a pair of special shoes that latched into the stage floor, letting the dancer's body slant forward without tipping over.

The Moonwalk

Technically called "the backslide", Michael enlisted a couple of top dancers from *Soul Train* to teach him the move where the dancer rolls backwards while his feet appear to be going forward. His debut of the manoeuvre in 1983 on the *Motown 25* television show was ranked by *TV Guide* as #2 on their "100 Moments That Rocked Television" list, just behind Bill Clinton and his sax on *The Arsenio Hall Show*.

The Zombie

The most recognisable move from the 'Thriller' film, the dancer forms his hands into a claw-like formation, raises arms perpendicular to the floor and swings them back and forth. It was a cheeky take on classic zombie gestures featured in films like *Night Of The Living Dead*. It has been replicated in sports arenas and wedding parties ever since.

The Robot

The move may have roots in the late sixties, but Michael adopted it after watching the dancers of *Soul Train* give it life in the seventies. The routine mixes classic mime with pop-and-lock and playfully mimics what it might look like if a funky mannequin had suddenly come to life.

En Pointe

Usually a technique performed by classically trained ballerinas, in simplest terms, it's when a dancer rises onto the very tip of his toes. Michael's use of it in 'Billie Jean', and the way the camera frame froze while he was still holding the position, was one of the factors that made the video such a huge hit on MTV.

Crotch Grab

Fans first got a peak at the goods when Michael added this move to his repertoire for the 'Bad' video. However, it wasn't until four years later that he got a severe tongue-lashing when 'Black Or White' premiered and showed Michael not only grabbing the family jewels but grinding while doing so. When asked about it by Oprah Winfrey in 1993, Michael answered

Super Spin

Michael began perfecting his spins ever since he was a little kid watching James Brown on television. He really started turning them out during the Jackson 5 routines of the mid-seventies. At his dancing peak, he was ending them en pointe or dropping to his knees while the number of rotations would often reach as high as five or six at a time.

Riding the
BOOGIE

THEY WERE GOIN' PLACES

It was while the Jackson family were proving themselves a profitable Vegas attraction that they decided it was time to leave Motown. The brothers, and especially Michael, had grown tired of singing the songs handed over to them by Berry Gordy's team. Like Motown's Stevie Wonder and Marvin Gaye, they wanted more creative control over their recordings and ached to write and produce. But Gordy would have none of it and refused to give the J5 a more active role in crafting their own music. So in the summer of 1975, Joseph rounded up the troops and held a press conference announcing that the Jackson 5 had signed a new contract with CBS/ Epic Records. Other changes included the name, which would now be simply The Jacksons since Motown owned the "Jackson 5" trademark. Jermaine, who was now married to Gordy's daughter Hazel, left the group in a show of solidarity with his new wife and father-in-law. He was replaced by Randy, who was now in his teens.

Above: The family gathers onstage in an episode of *The Jacksons* television series.
Right: Posing on motorcycles wearing flamboyant red and black stage costumes by Warden Neil, a costume designer who worked on the CBS show.

LABEL CHANGE

In the midst of the label change, and subsequent legal fight that occurred between Motown and the Jackson family, Joseph had agreed to take their Las Vegas act to Hollywood. Executives from CBS Television had seen the revue and thought it would translate well to television. So when network executives approached Joe with the idea, he jumped on it, much to the chagrin of young Michael. Although he feared that overexposure could hurt their record sales, he reluctantly signed the contract for a four-episode run in June 1976.

NOW IT'S THE JACKSONS

The Jacksons (as it was cleverly titled) was pretty representative of variety show television in the mid-seventies: musical numbers mixed with vaudevillian bits against a soundtrack of pop songs and show tunes backed by dreadful canned laughter. Each episode was bookended by segments of the brothers performing their past hits or latest releases in front of an enthusiastic studio audience. A massive "Jacksons" logo brightened up the background, covered in blinking runner lights which also bordered the stage. The skits were poorly written and shamefully cheesy, with one particularly ill-conceived sketch featuring the brothers and sisters portraying couples as Jackie sang a cover of Paul Simon's '50 Ways To Leave Your Lover'. Another had the family decked out as fifties greasers, in leather jackets and pompadour wigs, belting out a tune called 'Doing The Fonz' (as in Fonzi from *Happy Days*). Michael complained about the poor lighting, low quality sets and silly period costumes.

Although *The Jacksons* was the first of the variety genre to be hosted by an African American family, celebrity guest stars were usually older and white and appeared quite befuddled when attempting to dance next to the young, rhythmic Jackson kids. Unfortunately, the siblings seemed just as misplaced while trying their hands at sketch comedy; the jokes were lame and their comedic timing was lacking (with the exception of Janet, who seemed a natural and consequently attracted plenty of genuine laughs). *Laugh-In* it was not, and Michael knew it. Much to his dismay, however, the ratings that summer were good enough for CBS to order a new series of episodes as a mid-season replacement the following winter.

Above: Dancing together on *The Jacksons*.
Opposite: Variety shows like *The Jacksons* were a television staple in the 1970s. Here, Michael is making a guest appearance on *The Sonny & Cher Show* in 1976.

A MISERABLE TIME

The tight schedule he had to adhere to was another reason why *The Jacksons* was a miserable experience for Michael. Having to put together a new show each week meant less rehearsal time which made him feel too rushed and unable to perfect, amongst many things, the choreography. Not surprisingly, it was Michael's killer dance skills that made *The Jacksons* a must-watch event in spite of its flaws. The most enjoyable segments of the show were when Michael got to show off his footwork, whether he was chugging along to 'Dancing Machine' or hoofing it with tap dance legends the Nicholas Brothers. His range was impressive, especially for someone with no formal dance training. Whenever he put on a pair of Capezio shoes, he easily outshined his brothers, adding extra spins and bounces while maintaining a cutting precision that they could never have dreamed of achieving.

If Michael was unhappy, the viewer certainly couldn't tell (perhaps he was a better actor than he thought). So while he failed to emerge from *The Jacksons* as the world's next comic genius, he did demonstrate his continued evolution as an entertainer who was quickly outgrowing the narrow confines of a family act.

THE WIZ KID

Michael was able to break away from his family, if only temporarily, when he was cast in the film adaptation of *The Wiz*. The musical, based on L. Frank Baum's story *The Wonderful Wizard Of Oz*, featured an entirely black cast and was in the midst of enjoying a historic run on Broadway when Motown acquired the rights to produce a movie version. Michael loved the original stage production so when he got wind of the film project, his interest was piqued since he had always hoped to get involved with film. When he learned Diana Ross was already set to play Dorothy, his interest became determination.

MICHAEL AS THE SCARECROW

Despite the falling out between the Jacksons and Motown, both Berry Gordy, Jr. and Miss Ross encouraged Michael to try out for a part in the movie. Since his love of old Hollywood musicals bordered on obsessive, *The Wiz* appeared to be the perfect vehicle for MJ to make his big screen dream a reality. "I auditioned for the part of the Scarecrow because I thought his character best fit my style. I was too bouncy for the Tin Man and too light for the Lion," Michael later recounted.

It took director Sidney Lumet only a couple of days to offer Michael the part even though his initial choice was comic actor Jimmie Walker

of the television series *Good Times*. Michael packed his bags and headed to NYC for rehearsals. For the first time, he was away from his siblings and parents, living on his own with sister LaToya accompanying him for moral support.

NEW YORK

The Wiz was initially conceived as a small scale feature but quickly turned into a $24 million spectacle that went over budget just four days into filming. Sets were behemoth, salaries were inflated and the number of extras was excessive. Instead of Kansas, the "urban fantasy" was set in New York City with the Dorothy character now a Harlem schoolteacher. Shot in Manhattan, Brooklyn and Queens, production designer Tony Walton put an apocalyptic yet glossy spin on the city's celebrated landmarks, covering the Coney Island Cyclone roller coaster in yellow vinyl — for the brick road — and converting the New York State Pavilion World's Fair grounds into a glowing discofied Munchkin Land. The World Trade Center, lit up with 27,000 bulbs, doubled as Emerald City.

Above: Michael eases on down the road with the cast of *The Wiz*: Michael as the Scarecrow, Nipsey Russell as the Tin Man, Diana Ross as Dorothy and Ted Ross as the Lion.
Opposite: Michael's darling Scarecrow won over the critics (top), the theatrical poster (bottom left), Michael and Diana Ross at the film's press conference (bottom right).

FRIGHT WIG

Walton also designed the costumes, creating memorable looks for all of the central characters, like Michael's Scarecrow, which was cleverly inspired by the striped tops and golf knickers worn by popular street dance troupe the Lockers. Michael cherished his ensemble which included a "fright wig" made from steel wool pads and giant garbage bag body stuffed with philosophical quotations. Make-up was a tedious process, taking cosmetologist Stan Wilson four to five hours to apply to Michael's face every morning, a routine he actually looked forward to. So enamoured was he with his Scarecrow visage, he'd even wear the mask home at night after filming ended (troubled with acne, it was a welcome cover-up to the condition of his skin).

SHOWING UP DIANA

When it came to working on the dance routines, Michael easily learned the steps and even put his own stamp on the choreography. Inspired by one of his idols, Charlie Chaplin, Michael adopted mannerisms similar to that of the silent film star, bumbling along the yellow brick road duck-footed with his bendy legs collapsing beneath him, adding an endearingly clumsy affectation to every step. Diana Ross, however,

thought he learned the routines *too* quickly. While Michael intuitively picked up the choreography at the direction of the instructor, Ross wasn't possessed of such skills and told Michael as much. "You're embarrassing me," she scolded him. When she explained why she was agitated, he pretended to learn at a slower pace.

But impressive dancing, overblown sets and extravagant costuming couldn't save *The Wiz* from being universally panned by most film reviewers on its theatrical release in November 1978. Diana Ross was subjected to the most criticism; her hapless angst-ridden performance was compounded by the notion that she was way too old to play Dorothy in the first place. Commercially, *The Wiz* didn't fare any better, becoming a very expensive flop for Motown. The one bright spot was Michael, whose lovable portrayal of Scarecrow received accolades and indicated he would be a promising presence on the big screen (indeed, Michael impressed everyone on the set as well, learning not only his own lines and choreography, but everyone else's too). Shortly after *The Wiz* premiered, he was offered a role in another Broadway musical-turned-movie, *A Chorus Line*. However, the part was for a gay dancer named Paul and not wanting to fuel rumours that were already floating around the gossip pages, he turned the offer down.

One of Michael's idols was Charlie Chaplin. During a 1979 trip to London, he dressed up like the silent film star and posed for a series of pictures for photographer Tony Prime, who shot Michael in front of the Chaplin family home.

"I suppose many people would expect me to be very fashion-conscious, but all I need are a couple of shirts and some corduroy pants. I have almost no clothes, I don't even have a suit."

That is how Michael Jackson responded to a question about fashion back in 1979. Over time, he would continue to make that claim, that he only cared about his clothes when he was on stage. And it was true, especially during the seventies and eighties when his downtime style consisted mostly of cardigans, sweaters, and button-down shirts. Combine those pieces with his high-water hems and white socks, and the overall look was adorably nerdy, a curious departure from the razzmatazz that characterised his performance gear. However, when taking into consideration who he idolised, it is apparent that the spirit of his everyday wardrobe was pure Gene Kelly. Take a look at photos of Kelly during his heyday and a sweater vest, polo shirt or crew neck pullover is usually part of the picture.

One of the most ubiquitous promo photos of Michael from the eighties is also one of his preppiest moments. Michael chose a yellow sweater vest and bow-tie to top his otherwise white outfit for a 1983 picture session with young photographer Matthew Rolston. Rolston, just a handful of years out of college, had a habit of wearing fanciful rhinestone brooches with his jeans and T-shirts in that "ironic" way art school kids are prone to do. Michael, bemused, borrowed the jewellery to wear for the shoot, a last-minute stylistic decision that launched a teenybop fashion trend and sold several million posters.

The combination of casual wear and regal jewels is a style Rolston dubbed "Hollywood Royale" and would soon spark Michael's interest in dressing with aristocratic flair.

Opposite top: Michael in Japan, 1973.
Opposite bottom: Wearing a crested cardigan at home in California.
This page (clockwise): Collecting statues at the American Music Awards in 1981; Michael had a thing for blue sweaters; the famous yellow vest and bow tie; with Janet in 1977.

A DATE WITH DESTINY

Once the Jacksons' contract with Motown officially expired, CBS/Epic wasted no time getting its new stars back into the recording studio to see what kind of magic they could create. Assigned producers Kenneth Gamble and Leon Huff of CBS subsidiary label Philadelphia International Records, the boys' first two releases, *The Jacksons* and *Goin' Places*, were overall disappointments, but they did spawn a couple of moderately successful hit songs in the Philly soul tradition, most notably 'Enjoy Yourself' and 'Show You The Way To Go'. But the real achievement was that for the first time, Michael was allowed to contribute his own compositions, four of which made it to vinyl. By the time the Jacksons were ready to record their third record, Michael convinced CBS to take a bigger leap of faith and allow the group to produce an entire album on their own.

DESTINY

Released in late 1978, *Destiny* became the Jacksons' most successful album to date, attaining certified platinum status. Epic Records heralded it as "the first time in their [the Jacksons'] dazzling ten-year career that they have written or produced every song on an entire record". Though this might have been technically true, it was a little misleading; most of the behind-the-scenes work was done by executive producers, Bobby Colomby and Mike Atkinson. Soulful, exuberant and playful with ample grooves made for a booty bumpin' dance floor throwdown, *Destiny* was a critical and commercial sensation, described as a "musical coming-of-age" that brought the Jacksons back from the brink of obscurity. The driving success behind *Destiny* was the spectacular 'Shake Your Body (Down To The Ground)', a shimmery disco-funk anthem that sold over two- million copies and was a hint of things to come for Michael and his own sound.

VIDEOS & MTV

Destiny also marked Michael Jackson's debut performance in a music video. The birth of MTV was still over two years away, but the short film was already becoming a popular promotional tool in the music industry. By 1978, three-minute "pop clips" of current singles were airing as filler on television programmes like *The Midnight Special* or featured on *Video Concert Hall*, the USA Network show which broadcast an unhosted roster of musical shorts. Epic took a chance on the medium with *Destiny*'s first single, 'Blame It On The Boogie' and put it in the hands of director Peter Conn. The video was somewhat minimal, showcasing the Jacksons dancing and singing against a simple black background. Dizzying computer generated special effects were employed, like the glowing motion blurs that trailed the guys' movements. Image West studios in Los Angeles created the animated graphics which were revolutionary at the time and proved to be the perfect companion to Michael's dancing, which was all leg kicks and hip swivels.

MJ, sporting a boyish star-studded sweater vest and tee, was dressed far more modestly than his hunky, bare-chested brothers, a disparity that would continue for as long as the family performed together. He also appeared to be the most comfortable in front of the camera, a broad smile across his face and bouncing joyfully in every frame. The video didn't help 'Boogie' become a runaway hit — it peaked at number 54 on the *Billboard* chart — but it did give Michael a look at the process behind making a music video.

Above: A promotional photo of the newly renamed Jacksons, wearing Shakespearean, space-age designs by Bill Whitten.
Opposite: Michael, already tiring of performing with the family, seems to be hiding in the back under the giant orange umbrella.

10TH ANNIVERSARY

The Jacksons headed to Europe to launch a world tour which not only supported *Destiny* but doubled as an celebration of the group's 10th anniversary as recording artists. The concert industry had changed dramatically since the days of the Jackson 5. Touring shows were now akin to travelling circuses: bigger, brasher and more ostentatious that ever. Arena bands like Kiss and Parliament/Funkadelic led the way, turning rock concerts into sensory overloaded theatrical events with the addition of video screens, smoke machines, pyrotechnics, and elaborate costumes. The Jacksons' *Destiny* tour was much smaller in scale compared to the shows put on by P-Funk, but it did boast a fancy multi-level Lucite stage adorned with a giant 12-foot tall light-up peacock. The flashy fowl was in honour of Peacock Productions, the Jackson brothers' newly minted company that would represent them as composers, songwriters and arrangers. Michael had chosen the name after reading a newspaper piece about the exotic bird, becoming enchanted with the feathery plumage after the author described it as "all the colours of the rainbow on one body". It was intended that the new peacock logo and imagery be emblazoned on all future Jackson products. "We, like the peacock, try to integrate all races into one, through the love and power of music," was a quote attributed to Michael that appeared on the back of the album covers for *Destiny* and its follow-up, *Triumph*

SPACE CADETS

Most current sartorial decisions were made by the Jacksons' latest costume designer, Bill Whitten. Whitten, whose Workroom 27 custom shirt shop had opened a mere four years earlier, had quickly become the music industry's preferred couturier after being "discovered" by pop troubadour Neil Diamond. His client list soon looked like a Grammy nomination ballot, including members of the rock elite such as Elton John, Edgar Winter Group and Fleetwood Mac. But it was the adventurous get-ups he created for Jackson friends Earth, Wind & Fire and the Commodores that ultimately aligned him with the group. After working on four episodes of *The Jacksons* series, he was now not only suiting up the brothers for the *Destiny* tour, but for the countless TV appearances that came with supporting 'Shake Your Body'. Whitten outfitted the Jacksons in the quasi-seductive, space-cadet fashions that had come into favour as the world became immersed in the delirium surrounding *Star Wars*. Many of the ensembles looked as though Michael and company were waiting for the landing of the mothership: astronaut-inspired jumpsuits in metallic fabrics with extra shoulder padding and rings of Saturn-like edging. Whitten was particularly well-known for his fearless use of ornamentation, like head-to-toe mini mirrors or the laborious hand-beading which became his signature. The *Destiny* tour is also likely where Michael got his first taste of dressing in military garb; one set of colorful costumes featured embellished bandleader jackets with fringe epaulettes and rows of brass buttons.

Opposite (top and bottom right): On the road with the *Destiny* tour.
Opposite bottom left: With Aerosmith's Steven Tyler at a Studio 54 party in 1977.
Above: Peacock imagery was all over the Jacksons' albums and merchandise, including this *Destiny* tour programme from 1979.

LIFE AIN'T SO BAD AT ALL

The marathon *Destiny* world tour country-hopped for much of 1979 before taking a much-needed summer break to refuel for a second leg. Michael used this downtime effectively, completing work on his first solo album for Epic. Prior to the tour's commencement, Michael had teamed up with preeminent record producer Quincy Jones, whom he met on the set of *The Wiz*. Jones, the film's music supervisor, bonded with Michael one afternoon after correcting the singer's mispronunciation of the name Socrates. When searching for someone to produce his new record, Michael asked Quincy for any possible names and Jones eventually suggested himself. There was some haggling with execs at Epic; Q (as he was affectionately nicknamed) was known for his work on film scores and jazz records and not so much as a pop and dance man. But the label eventually relented and MJ and Q wasted little time before getting to work.

OFF THE WALL

Born from those sessions was *Off The Wall*, arguably the single greatest dance record ever recorded. Released on August 10, 1979, the mirror ball masterpiece launched four singles into the Top 10 — two of which topped the chart — and kept fans out dancing even as the last days of disco beckoned. It was chart-friendly, a critical favourite, a clubland monster. And it was *everywhere*. Reviews cited *Wall* as "sophisticated", with *Rolling Stone* going so far as to call it, "A triumph for producer Quincy Jones as well as for Michael Jackson... discofied post-Motown glamour at its classiest." Michael's ear for dance floor-worthy rhythms coupled with Q's classically trained jazz background created a pop-funk fusion that was a breath of fresh air at a time when disco had all but lost its lustre. Opening with the stealthy bass line intro for 'Don't Stop 'Til You Get Enough' over which Michael purrs "the force, it's got a lot of power", *Off The Wall* refuses to quit on its groove, that is until Michael declares on the closing number that it's time to "Burn this disco out!". *Off The Wall* invited fans into a glitter-dusted new world where that cutie J5 prodigy was now Michael Jackson, a sexy and magnetic musical dynamo who no longer sat at the kiddie table.

THE TUXEDO

Certainly, overhauling Michael's former child star facade was one of the main objectives when *Off The Wall* was initially being promoted. Even the swanky album jacket was designed with one idea in mind: to let fans know that everyone's favourite little brother was all grown up. Michael's management team took this to heart when considering the cover image. "The tuxedo was the overall game plan for the *Off The Wall* album and package," affirmed manager Ron Weisner. The tux, initially an idea conceived by cover designer Mike Salisbury, not only served to remind fans of Michael's maturation as a man and an artist, but it also dressed him up for his entrance into the next phase of his career, similar to other tuxedo-clad rites of passage like proms, weddings and graduations (it's an intriguing synchronicity between the release of *Off The Wall* and Michael celebrating his 21st birthday, which occurred only two weeks apart). The tuxedo itself was an Yves St. Laurent model designed for women that fit Michael's wispy physique perfectly. Salisbury also talked him into wearing penny loafers to emulate Gene Kelly in *An American In Paris*, though the white socks were all Michael's idea.

Above: Still a teen idol pin-up.
Opposite top left and right: The tuxedo became symbolic of Michael's growth as a performer. He wore one in concert as well as on the cover of *Off The Wall*.
Opposite bottom left: Michael also developed a taste for crystal-studded stage wear.
Opposite bottom right: Wearing a white suit, several years before his *Thriller* album.

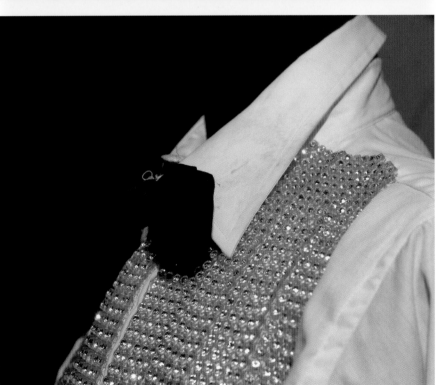

THE VIDEO STAR

This commitment to formal wear continued far beyond the album cover and right onto television screens when 'Don't Stop 'Til You Get Enough', *Off The Wall*'s debut single, also got the music video treatment. Directed by Nick Saxton, the concept replicated the bow-tied nattiness of the record jacket: Michael, dressed in the same glad rags he sported in that classic portrait, rocks on with his bad self in front of an ever-changing animated background of curiously nonsensical scenery. In a nod to Fred Astaire's 'Puttin' On The Ritz' number from the film *Blue Skies*, Michael even interacts with himself on screen as three MJs groove in unison. Dancing in a constant state of hip gyration with one hand in pocket, white socks flashing and sleeves casually pushed up, Michael created an indelible image that positioned him as one of the heppest cats in all of showbiz. 'Don't Stop' hit number one on the US singles charts just as the video started getting airplay and became Michael's first solo chart topper since 'Ben' way back in 1972.

SKATERS' ANTHEM

'Rock With You' was released as the second single from *Off The Wall* and followed 'Don't Stop 'Til You Get Enough' straight to the uppermost reaches of *Billboard*'s Hot 100. 'Rock With You' might have been slower in tempo but it was just as ubiquitous as its predecessor, another favourite with disco dancers and night clubbers. Roller skaters found the leisurely groove especially irresistible; in a 1980 American television profile on the Jackson family, journalist Sylvia Chase dubbed the song, "The skater's anthem in southern California."

MESMERISING

When it was time to film a 'Rock With You' video, Bruce Gowers came on to direct. Gowers was already an experienced player in the music video world even as the format was still in its infancy, previously working with Genesis and Queen, for whom he created the masterpiece vid for 'Bohemian Rhapsody'. In 'Rock With You', he nixed the oversized background graphics in favor of showing only Michael, backlit by a green strobe lamp and some twirling laser lights. Dancing as effortlessly as ever, the camera pans down to his feet and holds this position multiple times throughout the clip, making sure fans get a lingering glimpse of Michael's mesmerising footwork. No tuxedo this time either as Michael instead opted for a glimmering Bill Whitten original: tight black top and pants, covered in vertical stripes of rhinestone banding. On his feet are matching slouchy boots, also completely bedazzled in crystals, which only further emphasised those fanciful dance steps. The video gave a substantial nod to the not-yet-dead disco culture with its spinning lights and decadent costume choice. But it also had a bit of a futuristic vibe, signifying an impending new decade that was almost ready for showtime.

'She's Out Of My Life' was the third and final of Michael's video efforts for *Off The Wall*. The ballad, penned by songwriter Tom Bahler about an especially bad break-up, was one that Quincy Jones had initially intended for Frank Sinatra but he saw greater potential in having Michael record it instead. The vignette, again directed by Gowers, was extremely low-key: no rhinestone-encrusted costumes or colourful neon lights. Instead, Michael wears a blue crewneck sweater and sits on a wooden stool in another dark space. As he belts out the lonely lyrics and peers longingly into the camera, his raw emotion is palpable and it's as though he is about to cry, which is what he did while actually recording the song. It remains one of Michael's most poignant moments on record.

> **Michael created an indelible image that positioned him as one of the heppest cats in all of showbiz.**

Above: Going casual in the video for 'She's Out Of My Life'.
Opposite: Bill Whitten designed this rhinestone striped ensemble, which Michael wore on stage and in the 'Rock With You' video.

ON THE ROAD AGAIN

The *Destiny* world tour had only been quiet for three months but the Jacksons' musical world was turned upside down during that summer of 1979. Michael, who was already the most popular member of the group, absolutely *blew up* when 'Don't Stop 'Til You Get Enough' hit the radio airwaves. When it became clear that *Off The Wall* would become a behemoth of a hit record, on its way to selling 10 million copies, many aspects of the show were adjusted accordingly.

CRYSTAL-STUDDED

For starters, several tracks from *Off The Wall* were added to the set list. Gone was the giant Lite-Brite-style peacock prop piece which was swapped out for a "Jacksons" sign that hung above the stage. The entire family got haircuts, shearing down those once sizable Afros into smaller, closer cropped affairs that were now considered tres chic. Also done away with were the exaggerated theatrical costumes of the tour's first leg. Now, the stage wear consisted of more fashionable looks that came straight from Michael's increasingly popular video clips. While the star wore 'Rock With You''s crystal-studded ensemble, his brothers wore

variations of the Bill Whitten design. And of course, there was that tuxedo, which Michael (and only Michael) busted out to sing 'Don't Stop 'Til You Get Enough', as the omnipresent white beaded socks radiated beneath his cropped trousers. Wearing the clothes on stage that he had made so memorable in his videos was a conscious decision on Michael's part; he knew that the recognition factor would send concert audiences into a giddy frenzy. He even wore the tux for a Japanese commercial he cut in 1981 for Suzuki motor scooters which used 'Don't Stop' as the soundtrack.

By the end of the year, the *Destiny* tour was selling out most of its dates, setting attendance records and raking in almost $3 million, making it one of the highest grossing road shows of 1979. Not that long ago, things looked grim for the once mighty Jackson brothers who, verging on "Where are they now?" status, were having trouble filling Radio City Music Hall. But thanks to Michael and the lofty heights reached by *Off The Wall*, the Jacksons returned to the A-list and once again became one of the most sought after tickets in America.

Above and opposite: An array of outfits from the *Destiny* tour.

While in the midst of feverishly working to complete *Thriller* in 1982, Michael Jackson and Quincy Jones were approached by Steven Spielberg to produce *E.T. The Extra Terrestrial Storybook*, a spin-off LP which was part of the merchandise bonanza spawned from the blockbuster *E.T.* movie. Despite being severely crunched for time, Michael didn't hesitate to be involved. The project was incredibly laborious; Michael not only had to narrate a condensed version of the story, but also record a new song called 'Someone In The Dark', one of the most beautiful ballads he has ever sung. Nevertheless, Michael went to great lengths to complete the mission because *E.T.* held a very special spot in his heart; he closely identified with the saucer-eyed alien, saying, "He's in a strange place and wants to be accepted — which is a place I've found myself in many times... He gives love and wants love in return, which is me."

When publicity photos were taken for the *Storybook*, Michael delighted in interacting with his otherworldly soul-mate, hugging and talking to him, wowed by his realism and forgetting *E.T.* was merely a puppet (he even admitted to missing the creature after the picture session). Michael's poignant retelling of the *E.T.* story, along with the breathtaking new ballad, earned him a Grammy Award for "Best Recording For Children" in 1984.

Michael's emotional response to his play date with *E.T.* was indicative of his desire

to live in a parallel universe populated with colourful creatures and unusual animals. A self-proclaimed "fantasy fanatic", throughout his career he became involved in projects which allowed him to indulge his childlike imagination. The *Thriller* film, his musical take on the classic zombie flick, is of course, the most legendary of his accomplishments.

Underrated and lesser known is 1997's *Ghosts*, a 38- minute spook-fest in which MJ played a creepy Maestro who dances with ghosts. The *Victory* tour opened with a segment designed by Michael which featured eight-foot tall, lumbering medieval-inspired beasties called "Kreetons". Soon after, he shared screen time with a crew of screwball *Star Wars*-like critters for Disney's theme park attraction, *Captain EO*. Later on in the nineties, after seeing the cornucopia of wackadoo aliens that co-starred in *Men In Black*, he told the film's lead Will Smith, "If there is ever a *Men In Black 2*, I'm in that movie." Michael went on to cameo in the 2002 sequel wearing a fit black suit as a character named "Agent M".

But peculiar creatures were just part of the big picture as Michael also had a legendary affection for the kind of animals that weren't built from green felt and special effects. His heartfelt, Oscar-nominated rendition of the balled 'Ben' (1972) was the title song for an otherwise gloomy film about a sick, lonely boy who

befriends a rat. He lent his voice to another tearjerker 20 years later when he composed and performed 'Will You Be There' for *Free Willy*, a film in which a boy rescues a theme-park-dwelling orca whale and sets him free. That was followed by 'Childhood' from the sequel, *Free Willy 2: The Adventure Home*.

Michael always surrounded himself with numerous pets, beginning with rats of his own as a kid before graduating to more exotic animals as his collection expanded to include fawns, tropical birds, Louie the llama and a boa constrictor called Muscles the namesake of a song he produced for his friend, Diana Ross. In 1985, he adopted Bubbles, a young chimpanzee rescued from a Texas cancer lab who accompanied Michael on tour, sat with him at press conferences and wore complimentary outfits. His menagerie turned into a full blown private zoo after he relocated to Neverland Valley and a variety of tigers, giraffes, flamingos, and elephants moved onto the 2,800 acre property with him. And in one of his odder merchandise agreements, Michael's Pets hit the market in 1986, a line of plush toys which paid tribute to his love of animals.

"Anything that will take you off into another world... escapism... that's what I like," is how he explained this lifelong fascination with non-human companions before adding, "Fantasy, is what I try to create."

Opposite: Michael, Diana Ross, Bubbles and two little friends, backstage at one of the many LA dates on the *Bad* tour. **This page (clockwise):** Posing with a stuffed Kermit the Frog in 1978; replica E.T. figurines that once lived at Neverland Ranch; with his boa constrictor, Muscles; Michael's Pets was a toy collection released in 1986; with one of his llamas, along with brother Randy and an unidentified man.

SOCK IT TO HIM

It was during this time that Michael made several important accessory choices that would stick with him throughout the rest of his career. On the cover of *Off The Wall*, Michael is pictured in that elegant tuxedo, smiling and posing, seemingly mid-way through a dance move. The full head-to-toe image is revealed when the album jacket is unfolded, the bottom half of his body on the back. His thumbs, placed in his pockets, are purposely hiking up his trouser legs revealing a pair of white socks radiating around each ankle in an ethereal, halo-like glow.

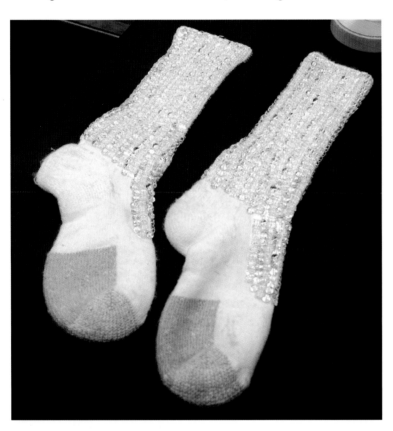

WHITE SOCKS

Like many of the creative choices Michael made throughout the years, the socks were a way for him to pay homage to his heroes, those

legendary triple-threats from the golden age of Hollywood. When paired with his tux, the look mimics Fred Astaire's oft-worn combo of a penguin suit with black shoes and white spats. In later years, Michael's white socks recall the more casually attired Gene Kelly, right down to the purposely high-water trousers and penny loafers.

Throughout his time with the Jacksons, his brothers would taunt him for wearing the socks, especially Jermaine who would even ask their mother Katherine to try to persuade Michael to take them off. But he never quit 'em, all the way through to the *Thriller*-era when everything he wore became a fashion trend, including white socks and short pants. "Those white socks must have caught on just to spite Jermaine," Michael joked. The embellished versions he sported on the cover of *Off The Wall* were created by Bob Mackie — Michael had been so dazzled by the beaded socks Mackie whipped up for Cher that he wanted a pair of his own. They also served a more logical purpose: to show off his feet while performing in arenas and stadiums, giving the folks sitting in the nosebleed sections an easier time following Michael's dance steps.

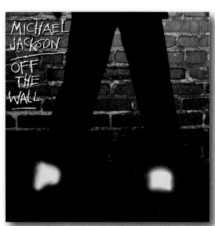

JHERI CURL

When a Special Edition of *Off The Wall* was issued on compact-disc in 2001, only the bottom half of the gatefold image, the portion illustrating Michael's legs and feet, was placed on the front cover of the new CD and inner booklet. On the back of the disc's case and inside the book are a series of photos, several of which show Michael in a tuxedo posing against a red brick wall. The photos are similar in spirit to the original shots for *Off The Wall* but are clearly not from the same session; Michael's hair is fashioned into a neater Jheri curl cut and his nose is somewhat slimmer. Perhaps all those years later, Michael, who was famously very picky about how he looked, was unhappy with the original cover art and decided to change things for the album's re-release on CD. Whatever the reason for the switch, he clearly must have enjoyed those splendid socks as they are featured just as prominently as ever.

Above left: This pair of Michael's socks sold for $60,000 in 2009.
Above right: When *Off The Wall* was reissued on CD, only the bottom half of Michael's body was on the cover.
Opposite: Those glittery socks were meant to be seen by fans up in the nosebleed seats.

A GLOVE STORY

Though the socks would go on to become a basic wardrobe necessity that Michael would wear for the rest of his career, they did not inspire urban legends of the highest order the same way that his white glove did. Stories claiming to be the truth behind the iconic crystal mitt are as varied as they are entertaining, with no shortage of people out there who want to take credit for it or think they know the truth. Was it designed to hide the early stages of Michael's vitiligo? Did he come up with the asymmetrical idea as a way to get people talking? Did a film production guy wearing white gloves inspire the look that launched a bazillion copies?

As Mike Salisbury remembers it, the white socks had been so outstanding in drawing the viewer's eye to those magnetic dancing feet that Michael's creative team began discussing the possibility of making gloves to match. However, Salisbury feared the completed look may be just a wee bit reminiscent of a mouse named Mickey so, "Between the agent and Michael and me, we whittled it down to one glitzy glove." This recounting of events makes even more sense considering the earliest photographs of Michael wearing that singular sensation were taken during the second leg of the *Destiny* tour in the fall of 1979, just months after *Wall* was released.

CHANGING HANDS

The glove would eventually go on to represent Michael's 'Billie Jean' persona, but during the concerts supporting *Destiny* and then *Triumph*, for Michael, it merely symbolised the magic of the stage show. It changed hands over the years, beginning on the right side in 1979, then to the left by 1981 only to return to the right side by 1984, and then back again later on. The construction and style of the glove evolved over the years, becoming more elaborate and complex. The original model (and the one he would wear on the *Motown 25* television special) was an off-the-rack racquetball glove with Velcro at the wrist and strips of rhinestone banding affixed onto the top only. The latter versions became more decadent, crafted of cotton with 1,200 round hand-sewn Austrian crystals on both sides of the hand. And although the colour of choice was usually white, Michael did opt for other hues on occasion — he regularly wore a sleek black variation during the *Triumph* tour.

"It's so show business, that one glove," Michael wrote in his autobiography. "I love wearing it."

Above: Michael was wearing the glove years before 'Billie Jean' and is seen here on stage in 1981 sporting a black version on his left hand. **Opposite (clockwise):** A close-up shows the extensive workmanship that went into each glove; Michael, wearing a white glove in 1979; designer Bill Whitten posing with one of his creations.

THE TRIALS OF TRIUMPH

There was no rest for the weary in Jacksonland so once the *Destiny* tour ended, Michael and company dashed right back into the recording studio to complete work on their next album, *Triumph*. Released in 1980, it turned out to be the last true Jacksons project where every brother fully participated in the production. *Triumph* was a bit of a departure from the Jacksons' past recordings; still danceable, but also slightly prog rock in its overall sound, with ambitious string arrangements, a robust horn section and operatic background vocals. Today, *Triumph* sounds a little dated and lacks the enduring timelessness of *Off The Wall* or even *Destiny*, but there are some choice cuts that stand the test of time, like 'Lovely One' and 'Heartbreak Hotel'. The most notable *Triumph* track is 'Can You Feel It?', which despite its mediocre performance on the charts, has grown some significant legs over time, including being picked as the unofficial theme song for the 2008 Presidential campaign for Barack Obama. More importantly though, what *Triumph* did is show just how much Michael had evolved not only as a songwriter but as a vocalist.

TOUCHED BY THE FORCE

The music video for 'Can You Feel It?' is a curiosity in its own right. Michael played a bigger role in its development than he had for past videos, supervising the production while Bruce Gowers again directed with expensive special effects by Robert Abel & Associates. The concept was the creation of the planet and unity of man with an introduction inspired by the opening credits for the film *2001: A Space Odyssey*. The video opens with a Kubrick-esque voice-over explaining the virtues of coming together in a world that is colour-blind. The Jacksons appear as warmly lit, golden god-like apparitions, their scenes interspersed with shots of waves crashing and fireballs shooting through outer space. With *The Empire Strikes Back* selling out in theaters, futuristic grand scale visual effects were all the rage and 'Can You Feel It?' certainly seems to have been touched by The Force. Unfortunately, the lightsaber sound stylings and loud blasts of thunder often drown out the actual music. Still, 'Can You Feel It?' has been heralded as a classic of the music video medium.

Michael singing his heart out on stage in 1981, wearing a variation of the 'Rock With You' costume designed by Bill Whitten.

ABRACADABRA

While the spirit of George Lucas is present in *Triumph*'s only video, it was Steven Spielberg's imagination that inspired the opening sequence for the supporting tour in '81. Each show opened with Randy inexplicably running across the stage wearing a suit of armour and carrying a torch, which led into a scene reminiscent of *Close Encounters Of The Third Kind*: rows of lights slowly arose from the dark like a UFO, only to reveal five heroes named Jackson awaiting their return to the mics. Always striving for perfection, the design of the set was closely monitored by Michael who wanted to create a show that could compete with the elaborate concerts put on by Earth, Wind & Fire, the biggest R&B concert draw in the business. Magician Doug Henning was contracted for his expertise in devising tricks of the abracadabra variety and orchestrated Michael's disappearing act at the end of 'Don't Stop 'Til You Get Enough'. But beyond the new optical illusions and extraterrestrial prop pieces, the show was more or less a visual and aural extension of the *Destiny* tour. The song list was very similar and included only three tunes from *Triumph* but a hefty five from Michael's *Off The Wall*. Bill Whitten's costumes for MJ were spun-off from the designs he created two years earlier for 'Rock With You' but upped the ante by meticulously covering knee pads, Capezio dance shoes and even an equestrian helmet in those trademark crystals.

SHOWSTOPPING

Sadly, the roadshow for *Triumph* was the closest Michael got to actually mounting a tour in support of *Off The Wall*, a task he should have taken on without his brothers in tow. *Off The Wall* catapulted him to a level of stardom surpassed only by Michael himself once the hysteria created by *Thriller* set in a few years later. The folks who filed into the arenas for those sold-out *Triumph* tour concerts might have considered themselves fans of the Jacksons, but it was Michael that everyone couldn't wait to see. Each night, his solo spots were the unquestionable showstopping moments and without him, Randy, Marlon, Jackie, and Tito would have been out of a job He vowed never to tour with his brothers again and in interviews with the music press alluded to leaving the group to pursue solo ventures full-time. His promise may not have been entirely truthful (the family successfully pressured him into the *Victory* tour in 1984) but it became a premonition that was helped along by the project he dove into once the *Triumph* tour finally came to a close.

> *Off The Wall* **catapulted him to a level of stardom surpassed only by Michael himself once the hysteria created by *Thriller* set in a few years later.**

Above: The *Triumph* album continued the peacock tradition, as seen on the back cover. **Opposite (clockwise):** Shimmering head-to-toe white; on TV with Diana Ross in 1981; crystal studding showed no bounds, whether it was on an equestrian helmet or pair of Capezio dance shoes.

Dreamed of being the ONE

STARLIGHT, STAR BRIGHT

Sessions for Michael Jackson's new album, initially entitled *Starlight*, commenced in mid-1982. Producer Quincy Jones and his "killer Q posse" of musicians from *Off The Wall* reported for duty. Though he was one of the most celebrated recording artists in the world, Michael was still feeling the sting dealt by the Grammy Awards voters who all but ignored *Off The Wall* in 1980 (not nominated for any of the top categories, his only win was for "Best R&B Male Vocal Performance"). When he returned to the recording studio he had one goal in mind: to not only surpass *Off The Wall* in sales, but to outsell all other albums ever recorded by every other artist, period.

McCARTNEY DUET

By this point, the fans and press had grown increasingly eager for new Michael Jackson music. Epic released 'The Girl Is Mine' in October 1982 as the warm-up act for the forthcoming new album. The saccharine yet catchy duet with Paul McCartney charted at number two even though critics were somewhat underwhelmed; many thought Michael had lost his edge. But the initial lack of excitement didn't last once the headliner, now called *Thriller*, was unleashed a month later to universal enthusiasm.

THRILLER

Unlike *Off The Wall*, whose overarching theme embraced a vibrant world that partied 'til dawn, *Thriller* was frenzied, aggressive and moody, surprising many who expected another joyful record from the guy who had previously told listeners to "get on the floor and dance with me". There were several frisky numbers on the album but it was Michael's own compositions that turned up the drama. At its core, *Thriller* was a collection of tales inspired by fits of paranoia ('Wanna Be Startin' Something'), survival on the street ('Beat It') and vindictive baby mamas ('Billie Jean'). But dark overtones notwithstanding, *Thriller* still had the miraculous ability to inspire even the most uncoordinated wallflower to get up and bust a move.

CAN I HAVE YOUR SUIT?

The image used on the cover of the *Thriller* jacket hints at the danceability of the tracks rather than the temperamental nature of the lyrics. Echoing the high gloss of *Off The Wall* but with more of a relaxed vibe, Michael is lounging about like a male model centrefold, wearing a fresh head of Jheri curls, a black zip pullover and white suit from menswear designer Rick Pallack. The suit actually belonged to the photographer, Dick Zimmerman, who was wearing it the day of the shoot. When Michael was uninspired by the clothing options brought in by the wardrobe stylist, he spied Zimmerman's get-up and asked, "That's the look I like, do we have anything like that?" The ensemble immediately recalls another dancing king of recent past: John Travolta in

Saturday Night Fever. The silhouette of Michael's suit was different, slouchier and more contemporary, but combined with the tiled mirrored

floor, black backdrop and otherworldly "glow", the similarities between the album art for *Thriller* and *Fever* are unmistakable. It was almost as if Michael was telling the world that a new hot-footed icon was taking over, out with the old disco, in with the new wave. He could also have been winking at the world record that he was so desperate to break; in 1982, the *Saturday Night Fever* soundtrack held the title of Top-Selling Album of All Time.

Above and opposite: The similarities between John Travolta's *Saturday Night Fever* ensemble and Michael's equally iconic *Thriller* suit are readily apparent.

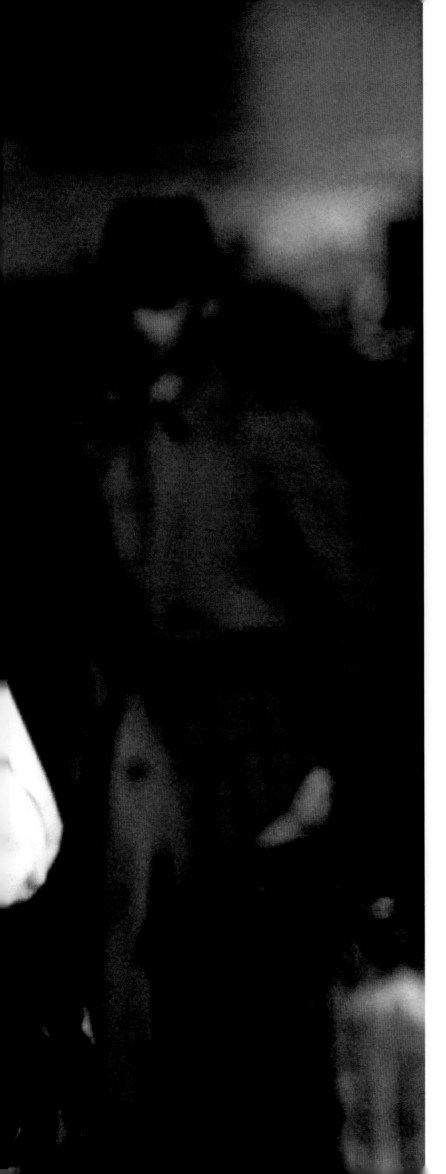

THE LEGEND OF BILLIE JEAN

The second release from the album and first to be accompanied by music video was 'Billie Jean', which hit the airwaves in January 1983. No longer just an optional media tool designed to help promote a song or album, the creation of video shorts had become mandatory for artists by the early eighties. MTV, at a mere two years old, was quickly becoming an important entity in the recording industry. The fledgling little cable channel aired nothing but videos 24 hours a day, making the visual and performance aspect of pop music of growing importance. But no one could have imagined just how important until Michael Jackson entered the picture.

When Epic records first presented 'Billie Jean' to MTV, they met with initial resistance. Network execs felt 'Billie' was "too urban" for its viewers, which they imagined as white suburban teens who wanted to hear mainstream rock and little else. It was rumoured that they relented only when CBS Records President Walter Yetnikoff threatened to pull all the label's artists from MTV's repertoire if the clip was ignored. Whatever the case, when 'Billie Jean' finally started airing, it was an instant smash with viewers and was promptly placed on MTV's coveted "heavy rotation" roster. 'Billie Jean' not only opened the door for other black artists to enter into MTV's orbit but it also triggered a lovely symbiotic relationship between MJ and MTV that launched man and network to unimaginable heights. "Michael and MTV rode each other to glory," is how Quincy Jones so perfectly described it.

> "Michael and MTV rode each other to glory."

LIKE KING MIDAS

Directed by Steve Barron, 'Billie Jean' opens in black-and-white to that haunting, minimal bass line and switches to colour once Michael's two-tone wingtip shoes enter the picture. Cameras follow as he slinks along a desolate city street, tiptoe-ing across a touch-sensitive sidewalk that lights up as he steps along, not unlike the multicoloured dance floor in *Saturday Night Fever*.

Like King Midas, everything he touches illuminates like gold: a lamp post, the stairway, a white-sheeted canopy bed. Wearing a slick black leather suit (another Rick Pallack design), pink shirt and red bow-tie, MJ plays the part of mysterious loner being chased by a trench-coated paparazzo determined to get his scoop.

The outfit almost acts as camouflage for the elusive singer, matching the cityscape backdrop which is also in shades of black and pink. And indeed, by the song's end, Michael outsmarts the stalker and disappears into thin air. Unlike the archaic, silly little band performance clips that previously made up the terrain of MTV, 'Billie Jean' was a thoughtful, well-crafted *short film* (as Michael called his videos) that had a plot line, central characters and mystifying choreography.

The dance moves were like nothing anyone had ever seen and it's inconceivable to think that Steve Barron tried to talk Michael out of including them. (Similarly, Quincy Jones failed in his attempt to cut down 'Billie''s 29 second intro when they were recording it; Michael insisted that it was essential to his dancing and won the argument.) The sprightly choreo was emphasised by Steve's freeze frame-style camera direction: Michael pops his collar, spins and lands on his toes in side-by-side still shots that left the audience in a semi-permanent state of awe that helped send the song straight to number one.

Opposite: Michael's black leather suit and pink shirt acted like camouflage in the 'Billie Jean' video.
Top: The handwritten lyrics for 'Billie Jean'.
Above: A T-shirt from the 1984 *Victory* tour, printed with an image of Michael in his "Billie Jean" threads.

> Like King Midas, everything he touches illuminates like gold: a lamp post, the stairway, a white-sheeted canopy bed.

AND THE BEAT WENT ON

As 'Billie Jean' was approaching the top spot of the singles chart, Epic released *Thriller*'s next single and short film, 'Beat It'. The video, budgeted at $150,000, was nearly five times the cost of the average music video in 1983, an expense taken care of by Michael when Epic refused to pay. The cast of dancers and extras was 80 strong, many of whom were from infamous Los Angeles-area gangs, the Crips and Bloods. With Bob Giraldi on directing duties, the plot for 'Beat It' tells the story of two combat-ready street gangs who are headed off to war in the concrete jungle. Michael plays the "mean streets Prince of Peace" who is out to prove that a meeting of the minds can be achieved through dance. He thrusts and pops from his dingy apartment to a diner, smoky pool hall and then to the garage where the rumble is to take place. Just as the fight begins, Michael thrusts himself between

the punks and convinces them that "it doesn't matter who's wrong or right", leading the crew into one of the most memorable ensemble dance numbers ever. Although Giraldi insists he wasn't inspired by *West Side Story*, the episode does have a Sharks vs. Jets sensibility with its two opposing cliques of synchronised hoofers, not to mention the fact that the phrase "Beat it!" is uttered at least half a dozen times throughout the screen version of *West Side Story*. In regards to how he choreographed the piece, Michael Peters explained, "The lyric dictated a lot of what the concept was... the dance continued to tell the story."

The large-scale dance routine was yet another element of old Hollywood musicals that Michael was the first to utilise in the pop clip format. And the kids were *loving it*. Endlessly spellbound, many turned their parents' living rooms into makeshift dance studios; after capturing 'Beat It' with their VCRs, the process began of rewinding, pausing and slowing down the tape to learn the steps.

Left: Finger-snapping for the big finale in 'Beat It', the dance number that changed the style of music videos. The clip's director, Bob Giraldi, denied he was inspired by *West Side Story*, but (as seen above) the similarities are hard to ignore.

And for those fans who lacked rhythm but still wanted to honour their idol, there were other ways to pay homage as 'Beat It''s costumes were ripe for imitation. Opening the video sporting skinny red trousers and a piano key T-shirt, Michael quickly changes before heading out the door wearing that iconic fire-engine red leather jacket designed by Rafi Weisman, a tailor at the Marc Laurent Paris clothing company. Worn atop a blue T-shirt with sleeves pushed up and paired with high-water straight-legged jeans, the head-to-toe look was a modernised, embellished version of the casual wear worn by *West Side Story*'s

gangs the night of the rumble. Festooned with gold zippers and metallic mesh piecework on the shoulders, the jacket was both blazing hot and endlessly cool, a seminal look for Michael as crimson became a popular fixture in his wardrobe from then on. Copycat jackets quickly became available on the mass market, shamelessly duplicated by high-end boutiques and cheap knock-off shops alike.

Several decades later, 'Beat It' fashions have attained classic status and reproductions of the jacket, the blue "Amour" T-shirt, as well as the piano key tee, are as easy to find today as they were back in '83.

> **Several decades later, 'Beat It' fashions have attained classic status...**

Top: A scene from the 'Beat It' video's mean streets.
Above left: The cherub and heart-covered muscle tee Michael wore beneath his red leather jacket.
Opposite: A young fan happily imitating his hero in 1984 (top left); actor Jamie Foxx wore a copy of the legendary jacket while paying homage to Michael at the BET Awards on June 28, 2009 (top right); a scene from *The Wedding Singer*, where Sammy (Allen Covert, seen here with Adam Sandler) proves that not everyone could carry off the 'Beat It' look with flair (bottom).

A MARVELLOUS NIGHT FOR A MOON DANCE

Thanks to back-to-back megahits, Michael found himself in the midst of an extended run at the top of the *Billboard* charts when on May 16, 1983, NBC aired *Motown 25: Yesterday, Today, And Forever* to an audience of 47 million people. The concert-style programme, taped almost two months earlier, saluted the label on its silver anniversary and featured performances by Stevie Wonder, Smokey Robinson, the Supremes, and the Temptations. Suzanne de Passe, now President of Motown and producer of the show, had invited Michael to appear with his brothers as a part of the Jackson 5, an offer he declined citing he wasn't interested in performing on television. Michael had a change of heart after Berry Gordy also offered him a solo spot to showcase his non-Motown hit, 'Billie Jean'.

"I LIKE THE NEW SONGS"
The night of the show, Michael and the reunited Jackson 5 sailed through a medley of their biggest hits, including 'I Want You Back', 'The Love You Save' and 'Never Can Say Goodbye'. More than ever, Michael stood apart from his brothers, cutting an especially striking figure as he led them through the songs. His body was slim and angular, contrasting greatly with their buff physiques. After the brothers exchanged hugs at the end of the set, Michael remained while the others exited stage-left. "Those were the good old days," he told the audience. "I like those songs a lot. But especially... I like the *new* songs."

From the opening riff of 'Billie Jean', the audience stood up and started whooping as if they knew that they were about to witness history. After slyly nabbing a black fedora from the side of the stage, he flipped it onto his head, grabbed his waistband, and thrust his pelvis to the cunning beat. After mock-grooming his hair and placing the invisible comb into his back pocket, he proceeded to lip-sync the 'Billie Jean' lyrics while popping, coasting and spinning his way to the interlude, where time seemed to freeze as he slid backwards clear across the stage. Dubbed "the Moonwalk", Michael later discussed picking up the sliding manoeuvre from "the street" when in actuality, he received a personal lesson from *Soul Train* dancers Jeffrey Daniel, Geron "Casper" Candidate and Cooley Jackson. But with a few tweaks (like rising *en pointe* at the end, a movement common in classical ballet), he branded the Moonwalk as his own. The entire routine was largely improvised and only briefly worked out the night before in his kitchen.

Above and opposite: The outfit Michael sported on the Motown anniversary special in 1983 became the uniform he wore whenever he performed 'Billie Jean' in concert throughout the Eighties and Nineties.

THE HAT

As for his undeniably boss ensemble, Michael put a modern twist on Fred Astaire by wearing short, loose-fitting trousers with a crystal beaded shirt, topped by a black sequin jacket that he had swiped from his mother's closet. The outfit helped to further separate him from his brothers who were outfitted in tight leather pants and see-through tops (the entire wardrobe set-up seems like a rather clever decision on Michael's part since he was the one who picked out everyone's clothes). The hat came into play when he imagined bringing the mystical narrative of the 'Billie Jean' film to life by wearing a spy's fedora, "Something a secret agent would wear... I wanted something sinister and special, a real slouchy kind of hat."

THE MAGIC GLOVE

Then of course, there was *the glove*. No one seemed to care when Michael wore single glittery gloves during the *Destiny* and *Triumph* tours but that was no longer the case after *Motown 25*. The white spangled mitt became the ultimate style signature of Michael Jackson, one that earned him the moniker "The Gloved One" and inspired a legion of cheap imitations to flood the accessories market. One manufacturer named Wonderglove was receiving weekly orders of around 10,000 for

their $15.99 copies. In New Jersey, Bound Brook High School officials were so distracted by their students' single-gloved hands, they banned them from the dress code. When Motown tried to ride Michael's coat tails in 1984, it released a Jackson 5 "greatest hits" album which included a white knit glove with "J5" printed onto it in gold. One reporter called the look, "the biggest craze since John Travolta's attire in *Saturday Night Fever* sent sales of three-piece suits soaring".

That magical white glove, combined with the hat, the clothes, and the dance steps that seemed to defy the laws of physics helped to establish Michael's *Motown 25* performance as important to the history of televised musical moments as the Beatles' US debut on *The Ed Sullivan Show* in 1964. The *NY Times* declared that Michael was "the heir apparent to the dazzling androgyny mantle once monopolised by Mick Jagger." When an impressed Sammy Davis Jr. revealed he was planning to parody Michael in his stage act, Michael gave him the black sequin jacket to wear for the gag. Madonna even playfully covered 'Billie Jean' on stage during her 1984 *Like A Virgin* tour. Most importantly to Michael, the day after the broadcast, Fred Astaire phoned him up and told him, "You're a hell of a mover." It was a compliment that Michael would go on to acknowledge as the greatest he ever received.

> In New Jersey, Bound Brook High School officials were so distracted by their students' single-gloved hands, they banned them from the dress code.

Above: At every *Victory* tour concert, Michael tossed out a black fedora into the audience.
Opposite top: Fans in the Eighties showing their love for MJ by wearing copycat gloves.
Opposite bottom right: The real thing, which sold at an auction in 2009 for over half a million dollars.
Opposite bottom left: Michael celebrating a winning night at the 1984 Grammy Awards.

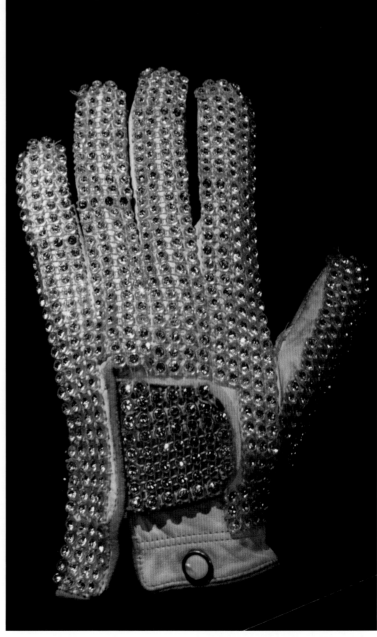

SAY WHAT?

The relationship between Michael Jackson and Paul McCartney began when the two met at a party in Hollywood sometime in the mid-seventies. After becoming friendly, Paul suggested that a song he had recently penned would be perfect for Michael to record. Entitled 'Girlfriend', the tune ended up on *Off The Wall* after Paul himself had recorded it with his band, Wings. Michael, wanting to return the favour, later phoned up Paul and asked him one simple question: "Do you want to make some hits?"

For several years in the early eighties, the seemingly odd couple spent a significant amount of time together professionally and socially. Michael conversed about art and music with Paul and his wife Linda at their English estate. Paul visited Michael in California as the duo watched cartoons and visited Disneyland. Their first artistic alliance was *Thriller*'s 'The Girl Is Mine', followed by 'Say, Say, Say' and 'The Man', both of which ended up on Paul's 1983 album, *Pipes Of Peace*. Just as 'The Girl Is Mine' was chosen as the first release from *Thriller*, 'Say, Say, Say' was picked to be the lead single from *Pipes Of Peace*. By the fall of 1983, the tune's success was barely in question as Michael's chart-topping prowess proved fairly impenetrable. (Case in point: 'Somebody's Watching Me', a song by the unknown singer Rockwell, son of Berry Gordy, Jr. Michael sang a snippet of the chorus as a favour to the young Gordy which helped send it to the *Billboard* Top 10 in 1984). 'Say, Say, Say' also came equipped with something that 'The Girl' didn't have: a video. A grandiose, $300,000 "Cassidy-Sundance romp" shot against an American Old West setting. Michael and Paul play "Mac & Jack", a pair of con artists who peddle a foggy orange concoction called "Wonder Potion" which promises supernatural strength to anyone who takes a swig. It's all a ruse, but Mac and Jack prove to be more Robin Hood than petty robbers as they use the swindled cash to buy gifts for orphaned children. As the twosome take to the stage in their very own Vaudeville show, Paul strums banjo and Michael does a funky quick-step while wearing straw boaters and wacky plaid suits from Gianni Versace. The buddy caper is peppy, if hokey, with Linda and LaToya Jackson making cameo appearances. "The egos could fill a room," is how director Bob Giraldo described the scene.

The addition of scripted dialogue to the 'Say, Say, Say' film was a feature that had not yet been seen in music videos and an idea that Michael expanded upon further in 'Thriller'. Also significant was the video's filming location, a town called Los Olivos in the Santa Ynez Valley of California. The small village of a mere 1,000 residents proved irresistible to Michael, who later purchased the Sycamore Ranch where he and Paul had stayed during filming and renamed it Neverland Valley.

'Say, Say, Say' was monumental, reaching number one in the US and number two in the UK thanks in part to the video which got constant airplay on MTV. Unfortunately, the collaboration was the last time Michael and Paul would work together. In 1985, Michael purchased the ATV Music catalogue which included over 200 Beatles songs by McCartney and John Lennon. For Michael, a lifelong Beatles fan, it was a dream come true. But for Paul, it was anything but; he now had to pay Michael every time he performed a Lennon/McCartney composition. The friendship soured, but after years of animosity, Paul eventually let his frustration go.

Surprisingly in 2010, 'Say, Say, Say' was ranked as "Michael Jackson's Biggest Hit" by *Billboard* magazine After tallying up weeks on the charts and length of time at number one, the publication cited that 'Say, Say, Say' had actually garnered a more impressive chart performance than any other Michael Jackson song, including even 'Billie Jean' and 'I'll Be There'.

THE MONSTER SMASH

"I want to turn into a monster. Can I do that?" That was the question Michael posed to director John Landis after approaching him to work on his latest project, a video for *Thriller*'s title track. It was the summer of 1983 and the album had already sold a remarkable eight million copies but was no longer holding the number one spot in *Billboard* magazine. A video for 'Thriller' wasn't initially part of the marketing plan

but when Michael expressed dissatisfaction at no longer being on top of the record charts, his manager Frank DiLeo suggested making a short film for the song to reel the public back in. "All you've got to do is sing, dance and make it scary," he told the singer. Within weeks, Michael was on the phone with Landis.

> "All you've got to do is sing, dance and make it scary."

GHOULFEST

Although Michael was not exactly a fan of horror flicks (too scary!), he liked the mix of comedy and gore in Landis' directorial triumph, *An American Werewolf In London*. He was also intrigued by the act of *metamorphosis*, a major element in the campy film. Landis, on the other hand, was familiar with Michael's video work but wasn't interested in slaving over a simple four-minute piece. He wanted to create something more complex with a comprehensive story arc and ghoulfest of supernatural proportions. Thus, it was decided to make this short film a little longer and more elaborate than the average music video. "We're trying to bring back the motion picture shorts," Michael said at the time. "I wanted 'Thriller' and 'Beat It' to be a stimulant for people to make better videos." But with this extended length came an extended budget, one that doubled the film's original estimated cost. Like 'Beat It', Epic refused to underwrite the project, reasoning that, while *Thriller* had gone platinum eight times over, its backslide down the charts made the time and money required for such an undertaking a complete waste. Michael, intent on bringing his vision to life, fronted some of the cost but, with the help of his lawyer John Branca, also devised a plan on how to cover the rest. Why not create a behind-the-scenes video about the creation of 'Thriller', one that can be sold to an increasingly rabid fan base? MTV and the Showtime cable channel liked the idea and split the financing while holding onto exclusive rights to televised airings. It was a solution for the ages.

THE 'THRILLER' FILM

Production on the 'Thriller' film lasted for 10 days with a cast and crew size that made the one from 'Beat It' seem rather pedestrian. There were two dozen dancers, 20 make-up artists, zombie extras, and detailed sets depicting a graveyard, retro cinema and broken down abandoned house, not to mention a team of technical experts needed to pull it all off. Landis brought with him special effects make-up genius Rick Baker, the "Monster Maker" from *American Werewolf* who acknowledged that his crew on 'Thriller' was the largest he had ever fronted. 'Thriller' also marked the first time that there was a female presence in one of Michael's videos. One of Landis' goals was for Michael to step away from his "Peter Pan" image, show some virility and take on a leading lady. Out of several dozen head shots, they chose actress/ex-*Playboy* Playmate Ola Ray to fill that role, a part that was originally offered to *Flashdance* actress Jennifer Beals who declined.

The video, which was loosely based on the 1957 cult film *I Was A Teenage Werewolf*, opens with Michael on a movie date with his sweetie, watching a retro horror flick about a boy (also played by Michael) who turns into a gnarly, werewolf-like monster. However, as the cinematic creepshow unfolds on the screen, the lovely Ray gets increasingly frightened and runs out of the cinema when teased by her man. Michael races to catch up and then coaxes her back into his favour by seductively singing, flirting and shimmying around her as they walk through the night, blissfully unaware of what was to unfold. Skipping past a graveyard hand-in-hand, they awaken its inhabitants, undead creatures that rise from their graves and circle the couple, ready to attack. But instead of being devoured, Michael himself turns into a pallid, yellow-eyed zombie. It's a freakish turn-of-events that leads to the climax of the film: a ghoulishly unforgettable dance number of rhythmically inclined corpses led by Michael who also co-choreographed the routine with Michael Peters of 'Beat It'.

Opposite: Michael and the undead, mugging for the camera.
Above: In full zombie make-up, with 'Thriller' director John Landis.

A BLOODCURDLING BEAST

When Michael told Rick Baker that he wished to morph into a bloodcurdling beast, Baker tried to talk him out of it by telling him how horrible the experience would be. Baker was surprised to learn that Michael had already grown to love prolonged makeover sessions after working on *The Wiz*. Aside from the deathly visage Michael wore while portraying a zombie, a series of masks was needed at various stages of the morphing process in order for the singer to seamlessly shapeshift from human being into the long-haired predator in the video's opening vignette. The transformation scene matches a similar one from *An American Werewolf In London* nearly shot-for-shot. The result is a truly startling on-screen metamorphosis that would be the first in a series of such actions throughout Michael's expansive catalogue of short films.

Costume designer Deborah Nadoolman Landis added a healthy dose of machismo to Michael's character, bulking up the slender waisted star by meticulously designing a jacket with strong shoulders and razor-sharp V-shaped silhouette accentuated by wide black edging along the yoke (cleverly, the additional stripes down the sleeves turn that "V" into an "M"). Nadoolman has explained how the colour-blocking doubly served as a "design element to evoke the DEVIL — chevrons are traditionally a fashion signature of evil!" The jacket also mimics the pyramid-like configuration of the ghouls who were dancing behind him. Red was the chosen colour because any other shade and Michael might get lost in the hazy graveyard shadows; red made him "pop". The matching pants were simply white jeans dyed scarlet. By contrast, movie date Ola wears bright blue, a leopard print jacket with cropped pedal pusher jeans and pumps, a retro *Grease*-era throwback that connects 'Thriller''s fifties film-within-a-film to the present day. Co-designer Kelly Kimball headed the zombie brigade, outfitting the cadaverous two-steppers in thrift store duds that were slashed, trashed and artfully destroyed.

THE GREATEST MUSIC VIDEO EVER MADE

Even before the 'Thriller' film debuted, the hype had been building for weeks with a red carpet premiere in Hollywood and MTV's inescapable commercials promoting it. So by the time 'Thriller' aired in December 1983, the kids were waiting with feverish anticipation by the television. And everyone was blown away. MTV started rerunning the 14-minute saga once an hour. The album jumped back to number one and tacked on an additional 14 million copies, at one point selling through an unreal *one-million copies in a single week*. Sales for the *Making Michael Jackson's Thriller* video were astonishing as well, shifting about nine million copies and winning a Grammy. 'Thriller' was cinematic musical perfection and to this day is regarded as The Greatest Music Video Ever Made. In 2009, it was inducted into the American National Film Registry of the Library of Congress, the first music video to be given the honour.

It didn't take long for *Thriller* to surpass *Saturday Night Fever* in sales and, according to the *Guinness Book Of World Records*, become the top selling album of all time, with some estimates suggesting it has topped 110 million copies worldwide. Seven out of the nine album tracks hit the Top 10, two of which made it to number one ('Billie Jean' and 'Beat It'). During the first eight months of 1984, MJ graced the covers of nearly 200 magazines. He was credited with single-handedly reviving an ailing music industry, lifting it out of a four-year slump by driving people to buy other records when they went out to buy his. There was also an increased interest in music by black artists; some have suggested that Prince's albums *1999* and *Purple Rain* benefited enormously from the popularity of *Thriller*. And finally, on February 28, 1984, Michael received a few of those little gold-plated trophies he so desperately coveted, winning a history-making eight Grammy Awards after being nominated for 12. Indeed, 1984 was looking like it would be the year of Michael Jackson.

In 2009, it was inducted into the American National Film Registry of the Library of Congress, the first music video to be given the honour.

Opposite left: Wooing his lovely leading lady, Ola Ray, in 'Thriller'.
Opposite right: A canister containing the prized film footage.
Top: Jaden Smith, Pharrell Williams and Paris Jackson prove that, even decades later, a good 'Thriller' jacket never goes out of style.
Above: Dancers getting their zombie on at the yearly dance-off, Thrill The World.
Right: Inmates at the Cebu Provincial Detention and Rehabilitation Center re-enact the 'Thriller' dance as part of a routine to keep physically and emotionally sound. The original video became a YouTube sensation in 2007.

THE NEW GENERATION GAP

During that celebrated Grammy broadcast, yet another highly anticipated moment in Michael's career was to take place, one that had nothing to do with winning awards. On the heels of a freshly inked $5.5 million endorsement deal with Pepsi-Cola, the Jacksons had filmed two new commercials for the company which were scheduled to debut during the show. It was a premiere greeted with the kind of fanfare usually reserved for major motion pictures with viewings at Lincoln Center and Radio City Music Hall in New York City. MTV even presented a half-hour behind-the-scenes special that centred around Bob Giraldi and his work on the commercials. For the spots, Michael rewrote the lyrics to 'Billie Jean', turning the song into a jingle called 'You're A Whole New Generation' which elaborated on the virtues of the carbonated drink. Fearing overexposure, Michael was initially against signing on to endorse Pepsi but as in many other matters, his family talked him into it. He agreed, but only on his terms, which meant that he would appear only briefly in each clip and have complete creative control over the final product.

THE PEPSI SHOOTS
The first advert featured a little gang of street dancing kids, carrying boom boxes and getting *down* on the corner. One of the boys, played by an 11-year-old Alfonso Ribeiro, was a mini-Michael decked out in 'Beat It' jacket and white glove with spot-on dance moves to match. While the rest of his brothers appear throughout the ad watching over the kids, Michael is not seen until the end when Ribeiro accidentally bumps into him midway through the Moonwalk. (Michael's brief appearance was obviously enough for the many fans who promptly hunted down copies of the graphic black and white leather Ted Shell jacket he was wearing.) The second clip was a concert-themed spot filmed inside LA's Shrine Auditorium in front of 4,000 fans. It opened with the Jackson brothers getting ready to go out on stage, getting dressed and made up. Again, Michael is separate from his brothers, his face not seen though there are shots of his glove, his sequin jacket and a quick peak of his penny loafered feet. He runs to meet up with his brothers on the stage singing "New Generation". When he finally makes it, he is still somewhat hidden, shown only from the neck up for about five seconds.

One comical anecdote from the day recalls a moment during filming when Michael excused himself to use the restroom. Seconds later, a terrifying scream erupted from behind the closed door. Larry Larson, one of the coordinators of the forthcoming *Victory* tour and on set for the Pepsi filming, ran frantically to the restroom, asking Michael what was wrong. The star sheepishly opened the door to reveal that he had dropped his very pricey, hand-beaded glove into the toilet. Laughter broke out as crew members began searching for a device to fish the mitt out of the john. Eventually, Michael just reached in and grabbed it himself, and then dried it with a hair dryer. As hilarious as the scene was, it did prove to be a bit of an omen of what was to come.

ON FIRE
Later on during that day, while in the middle of a scene where Michael was to run down stage steps amid a flurry of fireworks, director Bob Giraldi wasn't happy with what his camera was showing him. After several takes, he decided the problem was in the pyro, which he felt was seriously lacking in flash. After ordering more explosives, they began the fifth take as Michael again descended down the stairway. But while the sparks this time were definitely bigger, they were also overpowering, igniting Michael's hair which quickly went up in flames. Michael, initially unaware of what had happened, continued dancing until he felt the heat as crew members rushed onto the set to put the fire out. When paramedics arrived and began placing him on a stretcher, he refused to take off his glove which resulted in that famous photo of the star strapped to a gurney with his head bandaged, blanket covering his nose, and gloved hand waving to the cameras. Even moments after suffering second and third degree burns to the scalp, MJ was the consummate entertainer who knew a good photo-op when he saw it.

Above: Dancing in the streets for Pepsi, Michael and the kids bust a few familiar moves.
Left: In 2012, Pepsi resurrected MJ's image with a marketing campaign which placed his image on one-billion special edition cola cans.
Opposite top: Michael was rushed to hospital after being burned on the set.
Opposite bottom right: The Ted Shell leather jacket and shirt from the Pepsi ad, which sold at auction for $168,000.
Opposite bottom left: Michael with his Mini Me, Alfonso Ribeiro.

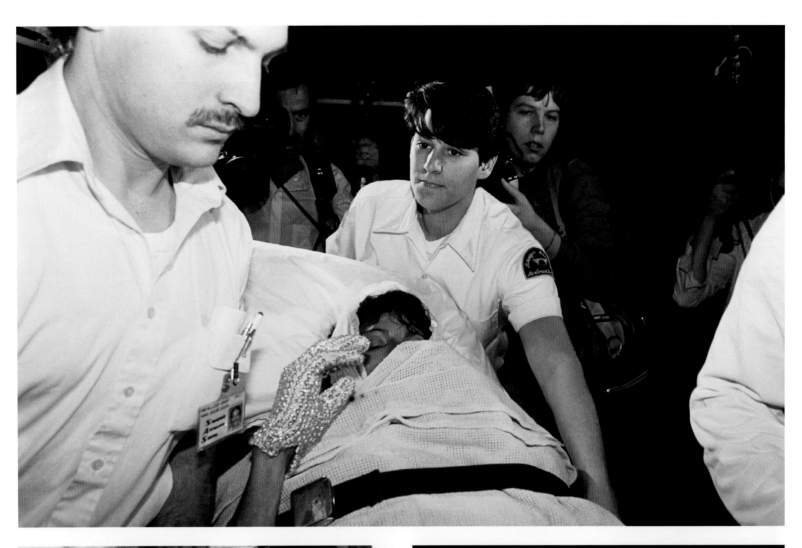

MICHAEL JACKSON STYLE *95*

Of all the iconic fashion statements Michael Jackson made throughout his life, it was the military jacket that he seemed most loyal to. Over the years, every new persona Michael added to the mix came dressed in a new version of the old style standard. There were the Bill Whitten crystal-bedecked versions in the eighties, the metallic Tompkins Bush numbers of the nineties, and in the 2000s, Michael headed straight for Balmain. And though the glitzy drum major models customised by his personal designers were the most

soft voice at the other end of the line belonged to Michael Jackson. After an apology-laden bit of small talk, Michael quickly jumped in and asked the real question that had been weighing heavily on his mind that evening: "I really like your jacket, the one with the gold on the front. Can you tell me where you got it?" A little thrown off by the question (Adam had been expecting to discuss a possible collaboration), he stumbled around for the answer until he remembered that it was a rental from Bermans & Nathans, a costume

playful, rebellious and one-of-a-kind. Palace guardsman and decorated officer's dress uniforms were an especially popular off-shoot of historical dressing; pieces adorned with rows of medals, brass buttons and braids commanded attention for the wearer, which was perfect for the stage. Along with the more casual army gear and battle fatigues which would also come into counterculture prominence, military togs were not only a subversive fashion statement, but a highly political one as well — a nod of ill will towards the

awe-inspiring, he wasn't above wearing pre-worn originals from army surplus stores or Hollywood costume houses.

The fixation seemed to begin during the period just before the release of *Thriller*, as evidenced by a comical late night phone conversation between him and British rocker Adam Ant. Michael had just seen Adam's video for 'Kings Of The Wild Frontier' (1980) and was not only entranced by the song's tom-tom beat, but also with the new wave singer's pirate-themed regalia. So with that in mind, Michael picked up the phone and gave Adam a ring, only to be unceremoniously hung up on. It was the middle of the night for a sleepy Mr. Ant, who thought that his bandmates were playing a prank on him. The scene repeated itself several times until Quincy Jones finally got on the phone and convinced Ant that, yes, the

house in London's Covent Garden. He also mentioned that actor David Hemmings had worn the exact piece in the film *The Charge Of The Light Brigade*, a bit of movie trivia that the film-obsessed Michael genuinely appreciated. After jotting down the correct name of the clothier ("Bowman's and who?"), Michael graciously thanked Adam and quipped, "Let's meet up next time you are in America, huh? Bye!" before the line abruptly went dead.

Michael may be more closely associated with the royal marching band look than any other entertainer, but he was just one of countless rock stars who embraced their inner soldier boy. By the mid-sixties, a taste for period costume had been growing amongst London's youthful trendies, who started digging through second-hand stores, antique markets and grandpa's attic in search of something

Vietnam War. Then there is the fact that they were cheap, plentiful and a surefire way to thumb one's nose at the establishment. Famous followers included Jimi Hendrix, the Yardbirds, and the Beatles, whose satin fringe-trimmed finery on the *Sgt. Pepper* album cover was the apex of this military costume trend. American bands Paul Revere & The Raiders and the Union Gap built entire acts around dressing like soldiers of the Revolutionary and Civil Wars, respectively. Even Liberace, unrivalled in his devotion to opulence, dazzled in shimmery epauletted wonders that were clearly precursors to those Michael would wear, a notion that Dennis Tompkins hinted at when once asked to describe Michael's style. His response? "Liberace has gone to war."

Opposite far left: Michael made a late night phone call to pop star Adam Ant to find out where he purchased his signature military jacket.

Opposite left: An early photo of Michael wearing a jacket seemingly identical to Ant's, circa 1981.

This page: A series of photos that reflect how Michael never tired of military garb, including a doll from the LJN Toys Michael Jackson doll line (above).

VICTORY'S SECRETS

The *Victory* tour was more a battle of wills than a celebration of artistic achievement. Michael wanted no part of the new Jacksons' album but like the Pepsi commercials, he was persuaded to participate after his brothers and parents ganged up against him and convinced him otherwise. *Thriller* was the biggest selling album ever and by all accounts, Michael should have been performing on his own. But he also wanted to keep peace within his family so he went against his better judgment and relented.

A press conference was held in NYC in the fall of 1983 to announce plans for a Jacksons reunion roadshow. The proceedings were led by the tour's loudmouth promoter, boxing impresario Don King, who boasted of the extravaganza that was to come, dubbing Michael the "golden voice of song".

THE UNWILLING SUPERSTAR

Michael sat beside his family, sullen and quiet as his brothers passed around the microphone. They were all clearly copping Michael's style, sporting the aviator shades and military gear that had become hallmarks of their superstar sibling. Following the event, however, nothing happened for months, which led to rumours and speculation with many industry insiders assuming that the show would never happen. Nevertheless, Michael's fans remained optimistic, taking it on themselves to launch campaigns hoping to lure him to their city to perform. Some 25,000 signatures were collected on a petition drawn up at Iowa State University. The *Boston Herald* printed coupons which encouraged fans to "Check this box if you want Michael Jackson to perform in Boston". Public pleas were made by mayors in Boston, Detroit, and of course Gary, Indiana, where a "Michael Jackson Come Home" event was held and included an MJ look-alike contest.

JACKSON & JAGGER

Dates for the *Victory* tour were finally announced in mid 1984, only a month before the opening date. Sharing the name of the latest Jacksons album, Michael initially wanted to call it "The Final Curtain", signifying his desire to never again tour as part of a family unit. But he was overruled. Outside of Michael's "State of Shock" duet with Rolling Stone Mick Jagger, his voice was barely present on the *Victory* album. He seemed to take a greater interest in the image on the album jacket, choosing artist Michael Whelen to execute the design because his work recalled that of painter Maxfield Parrish, whom Michael admired. The cover featured an illustration that suggested Michael wasn't particularly interested in being part of the group. His five brothers stand tall and proud with muscles gleaming, adopting a superhero stance wearing colorful, tight sexed-up clothing. By contrast, Michael, modestly dressed and less confident in his posture, stands way in the back as if he were trying to hide in the shadows. His glowing white glove and socks, however, give him away.

Above: Michael and his brothers at a press conference to announce their *Victory* tour plans in 1984.
Opposite top left: The cover image for *Victory* (as seen here on a *Right On* magazine cover), featured Michael hiding in the back, but his glowing socks gave him away.
Opposite top right: A rainbow coloured ticket for the Kansas City date of the tour.
Opposite bottom: An iridescent orange jumpsuit and reimagined 'Beat It' outfit were just two costumes worn for *Victory* performances.

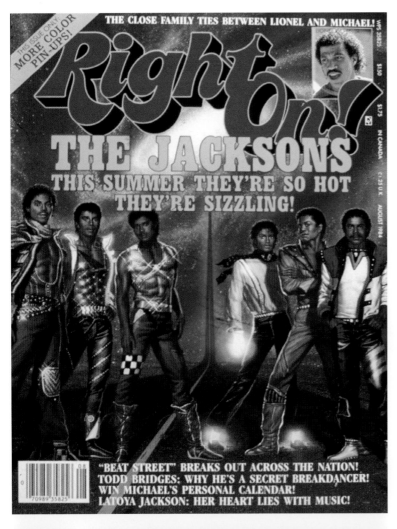

This page: Victory was theirs! Michael continued to cover up as his brothers bared their chests (top); a satin *Victory* tour crew jacket (middle left); designer Bill Whitten with costume sketches (middle right); and performing 'Beat It' with Eddie Van Halen (bottom).
Opposite: In a more low-key moment, Michael sings to a stadium of adoring fans.

SOLDIER BOYS

Michael was also absent from the two videos that were spawned from *Victory*, though his influence was certainly present. In 'Torture', a sci-fi S&M fantasy piece, the Jackson brothers-minus-one bare their sweaty, gym-worked pecs and abs while decked out in soldier boy finery, beaded jackets and mirrored shades. The guys writhe and grind their way through the five-and-a-half minute clip as animated skeletons Moonwalk and a white gloved hand magically disappears. By contrast, the peppy 'Body' features the brothers zipping around sunny Los Angeles auditioning leotard-clad jazzercisers for their new music video. Much of the choreography is straight out of Michael's playbook while the finale is awash in red, black and white complete with graphic set pieces and colour-blocked leather jackets. (Neither of these songs even landed on the show's set list which was devoid of any new material from the *Victory* album.)

A $16 MILLION SET

But whatever lack of interest Michael showed in the production of the album, he more than made up for when it came to the tour's design which he completely took over creatively. He surprised producer/tour coordinator Larry Larson one afternoon when Larson visited the star at his home to find him amid a large stack of story boards, drawings of costumes and stage scenery, all of which he had rendered himself. "Larry, I have a few ideas for the show." Larson made sure Michael got anything he wanted, which included laser beam lights, multicolour smoke bombs, Disneyland-like fireworks, and magical illusions, not to mention a $16 million set that took four months to complete. The overture each night was a more elaborate version of the opening scene from the *Triumph* tour with Randy again outfitted in head-to-toe medieval armour, running through a tree-lined *Sword In The Stone* themed set-up. There was also a parade of eight-foot tall Muppet-esque mechanical monsters called Kreetons and a scene in which Michael levitates into the air only to disappear at the hands of his younger brother.

SWAROVSKI CRYSTALS

Bill Whitten designed the $500,000 worth of costumes, a wardrobe full of outfits ranging from tuxedo shirts covered in Swarovski crystals to metallic rockabilly suits that were take-offs of Elvis Presley's early duds. A vast array of extravagant military jackets was created in rich brocades and lamé, meticulously hand-beaded then topped off with gilded sashes. Michael wore a glittery reproduction of the 'Beat It' red zipper jacket while performing the song, just as a black sequin blazer came into play for 'Billie Jean' (weighing in at 40 lbs, it was nearly a third of Michael's body weight). There was even a collaboration with Ted Shell, who built Michael a "suit of lights" and accompanying glove: encrusted with bugle beads and Austrian crystals, it hooked up to a nine-volt battery that powered the nifty 50 tiny lights sewn into it.

THE MADDEST HATTER

As well-executed as the costume plot was, it wasn't as if the wardrobe crew didn't have its moments of frustration, most notably the times Michael got so lost in performance, he'd rip off his jacket and launch it into the audience. "I'm sorry but I can't help it," he'd apologetically tell them. To compensate and help keep the loss of expensive garments down to a minimum, Michael would instead systematically throw one of his specially designed black fedoras into the crowd every night during 'Billie Jean'. Inside each hat were gold stamps that playfully read: "Made Expressly for Michael Jackson... 100% Genuine Fur... By the Maddest Hatter".

ONLY ONE STAR

Despite infighting between brothers, promoters and various entourage members, the conflicts during the *Victory* tour were well-hidden from public view, leaving critics impressed, at least with Michael's performances. *Billboard* magazine described him as an "all around entertainer in the tradition of Astaire or Garland". *Newsweek* praised his "gritty showmanship", and duly noted that "From start to close, there is only one real star of this show; it may be billed as a Jacksons tour, but it's Michael's all the way." When all was said and touring was done, *Victory*, like everything else King Michael touched, turned into box office gold, breaking all previous concert-revenue records by attracting the largest crowds ever and grossing over $90 million. However, this time, when Michael said, "I will never do this again" he meant it.

My friends you have seen NOTHING YET

ROCK & ROLL WITH YOU

Michael Jackson always knew what he wanted, and in 1987, he wanted to *rock*. "He kept asking me about rock bands," ace guitarist Steve Stevens recalled, to whom Michael also queried, "Do you know Mötley Crüe?"

When MJ and Quincy Jones reentered the studio to record the follow-up to *Thriller*, Michael wanted to go in a different direction artistically, one with a harder edge and fiercer sound. He was armed with over 60 newly written songs, half of which he wanted to include on a three-disc set. Q talked him out of such an undertaking and the pair whittled the list down to the 11 tunes that would end up on *Bad*.

Taking over two years to complete, *Bad* was introduced to the public at large via the CBS prime-time television programme, *Michael Jackson: The Magic Returns*. Officially released on August 25, 1987, lyrical themes expanded upon those which Michael had already covered in *Thriller*, feelings of isolation, social anxiety and predatory women. Musically, though, the infusion of more 'Beat It'-style rock'n'roll is what really separated Bad from its predecessor. On 'Dirty Diana' and 'Smooth Criminal', Michael's vocals were tinged with a fiery anger befitting his heavier sound while on 'Leave Me Alone', Michael struck back at the tabloid feeding frenzy that his life had become. Elsewhere, a passionate new swagger was unveiled on the soul-pop ditty 'The Way You Make Me Feel'. Then there's 'Man In The Mirror', which became Michael's introspective, gospel-backed anthem about improving oneself by looking within.

THE COLOUR OF HIS SKIN

The original photograph slated to grace the *Bad* album cover was also a departure from past albums and featured an eerie close-up of Michael's face superimposed with black lace as if he is wearing a mask. Gorgeous, gothic and a little twisted, CBS brass deemed it too bizarre for the record-buying public and axed the photo before it hit the printing press. The chosen image was an outtake from the 'Bad' video in which Michael is seen preening, peering seductively at the camera wearing a motorcycle jacket retrofitted with more hardware than an entire flock of Hell's Angels (the *Los Angeles Times* even asked its readers to guess how many buckles were on his outfit). The bad boy outfit contradicts his pretty face which was made up with smokey eyeliner and arched brows. His long hair and perky new nose lent even more feminine charms to the "new" Michael. The media began to obsess over his physical changes, relentlessly accusing him of everything from chiselling his face to resemble Diana Ross to bleaching his skin so he'd appear white. While some of the alterations were deliberate, like his cosmetic surgery, others were not, most notably his fairer complexion which was the result of an undisclosed case of vitiligo and foundation to even it out.

The original image for the *Bad* cover was an eerie photo of Michael with black lace covering his face (top left), but it was deemed too uncommercial. Instead, a photo of Michael in his black biker gear was used (top right and above).

THE 'BAD' VIDEO

The prime-time *Magic Returns* programme also debuted the short film for the title track, the first video release from the album. A Martin Scorsese-directed vehicle, 'Bad' took a month to shoot and was filmed on location in Harlem and on the Hoyt-Schermerhorn Station subway platform in Brooklyn, where coincidentally, Michael had also filmed a scene from *The Wiz*. The complete short outdid even 'Thriller' in length, clocking in at around 16 minutes though the entire video was rarely shown. Novelist Richard Price drafted a screenplay that was inspired by real life events surrounding an inner-city teenager who attended a private New England high school through a scholarship and is fatally wounded by an off-duty cop. Nothing quite so tragic happens in 'Bad', but Michael's character, Daryl, who hails from Harlem and attends an out-of-state prep school is loosely based on the teen. The film opens in black and white as Michael travels home from school to visit his mother and, on the way, encounters his old rabble-rousing pals, including ringleader Mini Max (played by then-unknown Wesley Snipes). Playful taunting between friends turns antagonistic as the group accuses their former friend of abandoning them for a richer life. Daryl realises he no longer fits in with the thuggish clique and decides to fight back. The scene then pops to colour and Michael quick-changes from his hoodie and jeans into his new persona as a black-clad wildcat. The camera slowly pans up from his feet revealing steel-toed boots, straps and buckles up his legs, a stack of chains and studded belts all topped with that biker jacket from the album cover.

Filming the music video for *Bad* on the streets (and below them) in New York City.

THE B-BOY, BIKE MESSENGER LOOK

Steve Stevens, a former member of Billy Idol's band who played on 'Dirty Diana', recalled, "When we met, I was wearing patent leather, he [Michael] was wearing penny loafers. I turned him onto the guy who did my clothes." Indeed, MJ's 'Bad' attire was more likely to land him on the pages of *Metal Mania* magazine than as an extra in *Mad Max*. But it was a strong visual transition that he continued in the surprisingly provocative video for 'Dirty Diana', which, with its stark spotlights, shredded curtains and wind machine, could easily have been a fixture on MTV's *Headbangers Ball*. Costume designer Rita Ryack, who had previously dressed Martin Scorsese's film *After Hours*, decked out the 'Bad' dance troupe in a "b-boy, bike messenger look" resulting in an overall visual effect that mashes Run DMC with *The Warriors*.

THE WEST SIDE STORY INFLUENCE

'Bad' showed a marked improvement in Michael's acting chops while his dancing was more technically sound than ever. His technique had become so polished, so nimble that unlike 'Beat It' and 'Thriller', replicating these latest steps with a VCR and remote control had become a much more arduous task for the fans. Perhaps as payback for teaching him how to do the backslide, Michael hired Jeffrey Daniel to compose the 'Bad' dance numbers along with co-choreographer Gregg Burge. This time there is no denying the influence of *West Side Story*, which Daniel and Burge were instructed to watch when setting up the routines. Many of the steps were lifted straight from Jerome Robbins' jazzy stylings but Daniel made sure to infuse them with contemporary street flavour, adding popping, breaking and Moonwalking roller skating. In one particularly memorable moment, the entire group performs what Daniel has dubbed the "Michael Jackson Scoot", a tricky forward-moving shuffle which had long been a part of Michael's solo act. But when executed by a large ensemble, it has the effect of "a train coming across the screen", not inappropriate for a vignette shot in a NYC subway station. Daniel, however, did not teach Michael the "crotch grab", which he also debuted in the video. The gesture eventually caused a furor amongst armchair moralists while many others were left simply scratching their heads in confusion (until a few years later when Madonna adopted the move as her own).

Opposite: Wearing coordinated colours with Eddie Murphy at the American Music Awards in 1989.
Above left: The buckle-laden gloves from the video.
Above right: A fan buying a copy of *Bad* on its release in 1987.

AMERICAN IDOLS

Though the choreography for his 'Bad' video might have solidified Michael's fondness for the film *West Side Story*, many of his melodic and visual influences date back even earlier on the Tinseltown timeline. It is no secret that he was a massive fan of the musicals from the Golden Age of Hollywood. Throughout his career, he mined old-time flicks, taking bits and pieces of his favourites and referencing them not only in his short films but also in his music. Gene Kelly and Fred Astaire were two of the most significant song-and-dance men in Michael's creative sphere; he dressed like them, danced like them, entertained like them. And nowhere can their presence be felt more than in the videos for 'The Way You Make Me Feel' and 'Smooth Criminal'.

Stylistically, the clip for 'The Way You Make Me Feel' is the antithesis of 'Bad', paired down and free of ornamentation (not a buckle in sight). Thematically, though, there are similarities, like being true to oneself despite feeling like an outcast. The full version of 'The Way You Make Me Feel' contained dialogue and additional scenes that were trimmed off before being show on television. The piece opens with a crew of loudmouth rude boys harassing women as they walk by on the street. Michael approaches the group, hoping to be accepted into their inner circle of jerkdom but is quickly dismissed only to be reminded by a wise old man on the street to "just be yourself". The advice empowers Michael who enthusiastically springs into action when he spies the object of his desire walking in his direction. Turning from shy outsider to swaggering Don Juan, he sings seductively to his lady love while chasing her through the alleys and side streets of a graffiti-covered neighborhood. She in turn, coyly rejects him until the end when the hero finally gets the girl.

AMERICAN CLASSICS

As Michael's fancy feet skip along the sidewalk and bounce atop automobiles so madly in love, one is reminded of Gene Kelly tapping on the street and twirling on lamp posts in *Singing In The Rain*; also contributing to the wet mood is a scene in which Michael's silhouette dances in front of an open fire hydrant. MJ's low-key sartorial choices also evoke the legendary hoofer. The unbuttoned shirt and tee combination, as well as his already ubiquitous short pants, white socks and Bass Weejun penny loafers, is a time-honoured combination that could easily have tumbled off the costume rack of Kelly classics *An American In Paris* and *Summer Stock*. The knotted sash belt was a nod to Fred Astaire, who regularly wore ties around his waist. So easy, the clothing seems like an afterthought, especially when compared to the complicated costumes of videos past. But as much consideration was put into this look as the biker outfit from 'Bad' making it another signature ensemble for Michael, one that he would resurrect often throughout the rest of his career. But if 'The Way You Make Me Feel' hints at Michael's affection for Kelly, then 'Smooth Criminal' is a full-on ode to Astaire.

Above: The grace and style of legendary hoofer Gene Kelly was an inspiration to Michael.
Opposite top and far right: Wearing the same outfit he wore in the video for 'The Way You Make Me Feel', Michael re-enacts the clip on stage during the *Bad* tour.
Opposite right: A pair of those famous penny loafers, waiting to be auctioned off.

CHICAGO UNDERWORLD

When the singer started conceptualising the plot for the 'Smooth Criminal' film, he handed over a copy of the track to master dancer Vincent Paterson to pick his brain for ideas. Michael had imagined 10 men in tuxedos, dancing in a swanky supper club. But after hearing the song, Paterson, who had previously danced in 'Beat It' and 'Thriller' and also choreographed 'The Way You Make', visualised a Chicago underworld hangout from the thirties filled with natty young gangsters and devilish femme fetales. It was an idea Michael couldn't refuse. Vincent used MJ's idolisation of Fred Astaire as the jumping off point, being particularly inspired by the 1953 film *The Band Wagon* and its "Girl Hunt" ballet sequence which features Astaire dancing a steamy pas de deux with actress Cyd Charisse. The vignette was a favourite of Michael's, one that he had previously referenced in 'Billie Jean'; the video's comic book-style skyline, animal skin rag and trench-coated stalker all have their roots in 'Girl Hunt'. But for 'Smooth Criminal', the correlation was unmistakable.

SPEAKEASY

Shot at Culver Studios in southern California, 'Smooth' boasted an industrial multi-level set built to resemble a warehouse-turned-speakeasy as well as a dance floor for several dozen hoofers. Colin Chilvers directed the scene, which was stocked with pool sharks and street hustlers in a diverse range of races and ethnicities. Vincent Paterson shared choreography responsibilities with Jeffrey Daniel, a fusion which would result in some of Michael's most innovative dance moves yet. Many of the Jazz Age-flavoured steps were drawn from the Astaire/Charisse routine, prompting Paterson to introduce partner-dancing to Michael, something he hadn't attempted since the days of *The Jacksons* television show. Paterson's Technicolor tricks were

interwoven with Daniel's masterful pops and slides as a spotlight follows Michael parading through Club 30s, across the dance floor, up to the catwalk, down the ladder stairs. As Michael arrives centre stage through a series of backslides and a tip of the hat, he and four henchmen carry out the anti-gravity lean, a move reminiscent of the Tin Man in *The Wizard Of Oz* and flawlessly accomplished with the help of harnesses, wires and clever editing.

THE ARMBAND

Of course, when actualising a suave take-off of one of Fred Astaire's most acclaimed roles, the star must be dressed for success and in this case, just like Astaire himself. 'Smooth Criminal' designer Michael Bush modernised the original ensemble from *The Band Wagon* and fine-tuned it for MJ's frame, cutting it slimmer and shortening the inseam, which also served to showcase his smart white spats and blue socks. Astaire's light grey suit was tailored instead in white with pinstripes which not only symbolised Michael's role as a "white knight" but also better explodes against the hazy blue atmosphere of the smoke-filled nightclub. The indigo shirt, white tie and hat combo were all lifted straight from "Girl Hunt", but also included were several novel new fashion details that were *all* Michael. There was the mysterious blue armband, which puzzled 'Smooth' screenwriter David Newman, leading him to wonder if Michael had rewritten his character as someone who was in mourning. After asking a crew member, "What's with this armband?" he was told the band was simply "Michael's new thing" aimed to enhance the mystique surrounding his gun-toting alter-ego. The same explanation was given for the peculiar white tape Michael affixed to his finger tips, though Vincent Paterson has also suggested that Michael dreamed up the idea after spying rock guitarists wearing Band Aids on their cut-up fingers, noting that Michael thought it looked "really cool".

Opposite: Fred Astaire with Cyd Charisse in *The Band Wagon* (above left); Astaire was the inspiration for Michael's character in 'Smooth Criminal' (above right); the "anti-gravity lean" was the centerpiece of the video (bottom)
Above left: A scene from 'Smooth Criminal'.
Above right: The white fedora from 'Smooth Criminal' became as iconic as the black version Michael wore for 'Billie Jean'.

Michael Jackson's schooling in the art of Walt Disney is legendary. An unparalleled fan of Disney features and shorts, he spent countless hours studying the history of the animation pioneer, reading any material he could get his hands on, and adopting Walt's creative vision and work ethic. "Walt Disney was a dreamer, like me," he would often muse. Disneyland was within driving distance of the Jackson family home in Encino so Michael took advantage and visited often. Dubbing the park his "favourite place on Earth", as an adult he would even entertain guests, friends and business associates by taking them to the majestic theme park, playing host to folks like Jackie Kennedy Onassis, the McCartneys, and John and Deborah Landis. He acquired an extensive memorabilia collection over the years and decorated his Neverland Ranch estate in themes based on Disney attractions. Hollywood mogul and former Disney

The Godfather director Francis Ford Coppola and co-screenwriter and producer Rusty Lemorande. It was Lemorande who had the ingenious idea to include in-theatre special effects, (wind, fibre optics, laser lights) and synchronise them with what was happening up on the screen. John Napier designed the sets and costumes and Jeffrey Hornaday, fresh off the set of *Flashdance*, orchestrated the choreography.

The storyline takes Captain EO (born from the name of Eos, the Greek Goddess of Dawn) and his "ragtag band" of creature companions across the cosmos to complete a special mission: deliver a gift to the Supreme Leader, a sinister claw-handed queen who resides on the dystopian Dark Planet. EO is desperate to please his boss, Commander Hog (Dick Shawn), who is losing patience and gives the crew one last chance to redeem themselves after bungling their last

alike robot Major Domo, his buddy Minor Domo, the ship's two-headed navigator The Geex, the Ewok-esque Fuzzball, and Hooter, an elephant-like character cut from the same cloth as Max Rebo of *Star Wars*. The ominous, post-apocalyptic landscape of the Dark Planet was imagined as the melding together of industrialism and Fascism. Michael suits up in a Stormtrooper-style ensemble with a broad-shouldered gold-studded jacket paired and trousers so tight his dancing becomes even more impressive.

The estimated cost for *Captain EO*'s 17 minutes ran as high as $20 million which gave it the dubious distinction as being the most expensive film ever made, per minute. *EO* played in all of Disney's theme parks, where special theatres were built specifically to house the attraction. It debuted at Epcot Center's Imagination Pavilion in Orlando, Florida on September 12, 1986 and four days later at the Magic

chairman Michael Eisner once described Michael as the studio's preeminent aficionado, noting that MJ knew "more about Walt Disney than anybody who ever existed. He certainly knows more than I do."

In early 1984, Michael and Disney had begun talking about a merger between Mouse & Moonwalker. "We wanted to create something with Michael Jackson, who appealed to teenagers, but also to young kids, and even their parents," clarified the Disney CEO. A new attraction was already in the early development phases, a sci-fi adventure called *Captain EO* that would combine 3-D film technology with Disney-style good vs. evil storytelling. In Eisner's eyes, MJ was the natural choice to lead the vehicle and when he approached the singer, Michael was receptive but would only do it on one condition: "Only if you can get George Lucas to protect me." Lucas, who was already working with Disney on a similar ride called Star Tours, came aboard as Executive Producer and brought with him

assignment. However, the mission goes haywire when the Supreme Leader (an unrecognisable Anjelica Huston, who hangs precariously from web-like rubber cables) turns out to be a bona fide witch queen who doesn't take kindly to good intentions. She sentences EO to her dungeon and his creatures to be turned into trash cans. But before he is captured, the Captain proves that evil can be conquered by music and love by launching into a song and dance routine, magically turning the Dark Planet's gloomy guards into an orange and yellow jumpsuit-wearing dance ensemble. The queen is transformed from hideous creature to beautiful goddess; her headquarters become an idyllic Greek palace. Michael performed two new songs in *Captain EO*, 'We Are Here To Change The World' and a pre-*Bad* version of 'Another Part Of Me'.

The George Lucas touch is apparent from the opening scene, when a huge chunk of rock is sent spiralling through space. EO's posse includes Yoda sound-

Eye Theater in Disneyland Anaheim where, to celebrate the film's release, the park stayed open for 36 hours straight. After the attraction's popularity waned in the nineties, each park quietly closed the production, with the final showing at Disneyland Paris in 1998. However the adventure returned to Disneyland for a so-called "limited engagement" in February 2010 following its growing popularity via YouTube and a petition from fans of both Michael Jackson and Disney. Retitled *Captain EO Tribute*, the film proved to be just as successful the second time around, pulling in an estimated 15,000-16,000 viewers daily (up from a mere 2,000 who showed up to watch *Honey, I Shrunk The Audience*, the flick it replaced). For the folks at Disney, it was a no-brainer to bring back *EO* to all of its locations and within months, *EO* was relaunched in Paris, Tokyo, and finally, Orlando, where the original 1986 marquees were found in pristine condition, dusted off and nostalgically reused.

WE ARE HERE TO CHANGE THE WORLD.

GEORGE LUCAS presents A 3-D MUSICAL MOTION PICTURE SPACE ADVENTURE.
Directed by FRANCIS COPPOLA Starring MICHAEL JACKSON as CAPTAIN EO
PRESENTED BY THE EASTMAN KODAK COMPANY AT DISNEYLAND AND
WALT DISNEY WORLD EPCOT CENTER ... AND NOWHERE ELSE IN THE UNIVERSE!

Opposite: Michael, with George Lucas and Francis Ford Coppola, on the set of *Captain EO.*
Top left and bottom left: Michael's EO costume had more than a few shades of *Star Wars* in it.
Bottom right: Pop star Justin Bieber and TV host Ryan Seacrest celebrate

BAD, BADDER, BADDEST

Immediately following the release of *Bad*, Michael set out on his most ambitious concert tour yet and the first without his family. Literally circling the planet, the roadshow hit four continents, 16 countries, played 125 shows, and took place over the course of a year and a half. The opening dates in Tokyo created pandemonium, with 400,000 tickets selling out in four hours. Not to be outdone, England joined in on the crazy when 500,000 people attended seven sold-out nights at Wembley Stadium. Along the way, Michael seemed to have a new nickname bestowed upon him at every stop; in Australia he was "Crocodile Jackson", the Japanese dubbed him "Typhoon Michael" while the English preferred "The Earl of Whirl".

STAGING THE VIDEOS

On stage, Michael continued the tradition of saluting his music videos, elaborately re-staging them into scenes worthy of a Broadway musical revue.

The climactic knife-fight in 'Beat It' was reenacted just as scenes from 'Smooth Criminal' had gambling men and machine guns. For 'The Way You Make Me Feel', Michael sauntered across the stage, chasing his (not-yet-famous) back-up singer Sheryl Crow, who teases while wearing the teeniest black mini dress allowed by law. And of course there was 'Thriller', complete with letterman's jacket, hairy werewolf mask and corpse-like ensemble. The live re-imagining of his film clips required over 700 lights, 100 speakers, 70 costumes, and one disappearing act, orchestrated by illusionists Siegfried & Roy. Michael and designer Michael Bush also made sure to stay true to the new 'Bad' image, keeping the wardrobe heavy on the metal, overloading garments with studs, buckles and rows of silver officer badges up Michael's trouser legs. Space-age elements were added to the mix with silver spandex, fiber-optic headdresses and astronaut-style jumpsuits, one of which, with its multiple straps and studding, could have also been inspired by the in-patients of *One Flew Over The Cuckoo's Nest*.

> **The opening dates in Tokyo created pandemonium, with 400,000 tickets selling out in four hours.**

A few from the road: Michael onstage during the *Bad* world tour, which ran from 1987 to 1989. The costumes mixed up elements from many of his short films.

BEYOND THE MUSIC

Just as Michael was coming down from the Bad world tour, he was gearing up for the unveiling of two new high-profile projects that reached outside of the record industry. First up was the release of *Moonwalker*, the $27 million film he wrote, produced and financed on his own and shot intermittently over the course of two years. The flick had a successful theatrical run in Japan and Europe but due to contract disputes with distributors, was released straight-to-video in the United States, where it went on to surpass *Making Michael Jackson's Thriller* in sales figures.

MOONWALKER

Moonwalker is part career retrospective and part short story collection bookended by live concert performances. The centrepiece of the film is the complete 40-minute version of the 'Smooth Criminal' video which initially wasn't even supposed to be included. The storyline is more extensive, setting up Michael as a knight in white gabardine saving the children from Mr. Big, a drug pushing overlord played by Joe Pesci. It was the 'Smooth' segment that was used as inspiration for the Sega Genesis Moonwalker video game in which a zoot-suited Michael fights bad guys with spins, kicks and a glittery trail of dust called "Dance Magic".

BADDER

Outside of 'Smooth Criminal', there isn't much of a cohesive narrative woven through the 90-minute movie with the only continuous thread being Michael himself. The vignettes are all slightly nonsensical, bouncing from loony animation and self-parody to crime thriller and science fiction. Michael satirises himself with "Badder", a comedic pint-sized take on the 'Bad' video starring a four-foot tall MJ look-alike backed by a dancing cast of grammar school kids. In the stop-motion sequence for the tune "Speed Demon", Michael dresses up as a mischievous Claymation Harley-riding rabbit with the powers of transmogrification. For 'Leave Me Alone' Michael is presented as both childlike and tragic, lampooning the negative tabloid press while cruising through a cut'n'paste amusement park riding a shiny green rocket ship. A technique called "cutout animation" was used to give the video a surrealistic feel as Michael is not only a kid on a carnival ride but also the carnival itself — a modern-day Gulliver, trapped beneath the curvy tracks of a roller coaster, who breaks free at the end just as Gulliver did from his Lilliputian captors. 'Leave Me Alone' took director Jim Blashfield and a 25-man production crew six months to complete. The hard work paid off, though, when the clip won a Grammy in 1990 for "Best Music Video, Short Form".

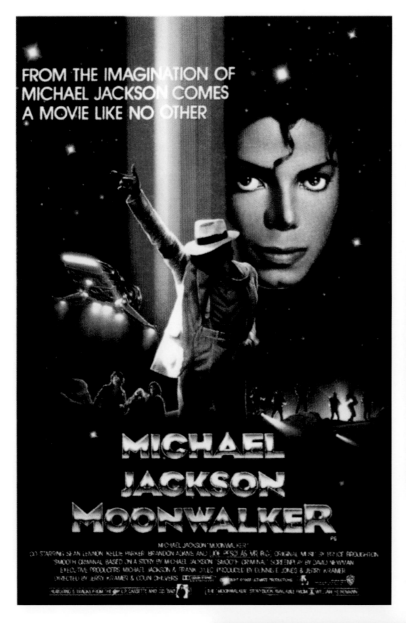

FROM THE IMAGINATION OF
MICHAEL JACKSON COMES
A MOVIE LIKE NO OTHER

MICHAEL
JACKSON
MOONWALKER

Opposite top: The film *Moonwalker* contained a series of unrelated short films, including 'Badder', which was a comical version with children of the 'Bad' video.
Opposite bottom: A robotic mask used in the film.
Above: The official poster for *Moonwalker* (top left); shooting 'Leave Me Alone' (top right)
Right: Michael dances with the Elephant Man's bones, also from 'Leave Me Alone', spoofing the rumour that he had once tried to buy them.

LA GEAR

Also on the agenda was Michael's collaboration with footwear company LA Gear. Many clothing items had become Michael Jackson style signatures by the late eighties: the black fedora, the military jacket, the white glove. On his feet, he almost always sported one of his many pairs of black leather penny loafers and rarely wore anything else, especially not sneakers. In fact, it is nearly impossible to find a photograph of Michael in athletic shoes. Even while playing basketball with Michael Jordan in the 'Jam' video, he didn't stray from his trusty Bass Weejuns. Therefore, his brief partnership with LA Gear seems all the more peculiar.

In September 1989, Michael and the sneaker company announced an unprecedented merger through an endorsement deal which would net the singer $10 million. At an awkward Hollywood press conference in front of an international media crowd, a predictably close-mouthed Michael, with a company executive by his side, said merely, "I am very happy to be a part of the LA Gear magic and I hope we have a very rewarding, successful career." The contract stipulated that after helping design the collection, Michael would wear the shoes in three of his short films. LA Gear would handle all areas of production and have the right to use his image and name for marketing purposes.

SHREDDED JEANS

The range was ready for back-to-school season the following year and was launched with an intriguing television spot which showed Michael's feet walking down a dark alleyway, his silhouette dancing against the foggy low-lit landscape. There was no music or dialogue, only the sound of rubber soles on blacktop and Michael's heavy breathing followed by a high-pitched scream which shattered a street lamp. As in the Pepsi commercials of 1984, his face was seen only for a few seconds at the end. The accompanying series of print ads starred Michael with a gang of grammar school rugrats posing with attitude in what appears to be an auto body shop.

Loosely continuing on with the biker theme started with *Bad*, he paired his LA Gears with strategically shredded blue jeans (an anomaly for Michael) and various metal-plated jackets designed by Tompkins Bush, including one completely covered in shrunken licence plates. The sneakers themselves were available in several models and in various combinations of black and white. With spirited names like "Street Magic" and "Moon Rocker", there was also the memorable "Billie" which had multiple straps, buckles, and studs, clearly fashioned after Michael's 'Bad' rockstar personage. The $80 sneakers all had the "MJ Moonwalker" logo embroidered on the tongues and branded on a tiny plate attached to the sides.

The "Unstoppable" collection was especially popular in the Japanese

market, with sales so brisk they made up for the mediocre performance in the United States. Still, LA Gear filed a lawsuit for breach of contract when Michael didn't live up to his end of the deal, most notably failing to

wear the sneakers in his videos. Michael eventually countersued with similar grievances. Nowadays, though, the original "Moon Rockers" and "Billies" are highly sought after on the vintage sneaker market, sometimes fetching several hundred dollars a pair to savvy collectors and fans.

> **Michael and the sneaker company announced an unprecedented merger through an endorsement deal which would net the singer $10 million.**

Above: A magazine ad for Michael's 'Unstoppable' LA Gear sneaker collection from 1990.
Opposite (clockwise): Michael with LA Gear Executive Vice President Sandy Saemann, at the press conference to announce the alliance; an LA Gear promotional photo; the license plate-covered jacket Michael wore in the print ad; the buckle-covered 'Billie Jean' sneaker was actually more 'Bad'-like in its style.

The extent to which Michael Jackson adored video games wasn't really common knowledge until a great portion of his gaming collection was to be auctioned off in April of 2009. An assemblage that included over 100 pinball machines, arcade cabinets and video adventures, it spanned across 60 of one Julien's auction catalogue and the entire floor of an abandoned department store during a pre-sale public exhibition. Fellow gamers flipped through the pages, filled with classics like Ms. Pacman, Jambo! Safari, Donkey Kong and Mortal Kombat, and drooled with envy. The sale was later cancelled, however, when Michael had a change of heart about selling off his possessions. Still, those images are reminders of Michael's reputation for being a "big kid". And to those who befriended him, he was also known to be a die-hard gamer. In the nineties, he had developed a particularly close relationship with the Sega corporation after the release of his *Moonwalker* game and spent a substantial amount of time hanging around the company's headquarters in Redwood City, California learning about the gaming industry. He had even considered releasing a follow-up album to 2001's *Invincible* in video game format. That never happened, but there were several contributions he did make that ended up immortalised in other games over the years.

Developed as a promotional tie-in to his feature film of the same name, *Moonwalker* (1990) was created by Sega as a game for its Genesis home console as well as in classic cabinet mode to be played in arcades. Loosely resurrecting the plot line from the 'Smooth Criminal' clip, the gamer suits up in white to play Michael as he fights through four levels of caverns and nightclubs rescuing the children from the vile Mr. Big. He knocks off bad guys not with punches and machine guns, but with leg kicks and super spins, propelling a trail of glittery stardust called "Dance Magic" whenever executing such a move, yelling "whoo-hoo!". Digitised midi-versions of songs like "Smooth Criminal" and "Bad" serve as soundtrack material throughout playtime. Bubbles the chimp even makes a cameo in the arcade version.

In *Space Channel 5*, a rhythm-based game created for Sega's Dreamcast system in 1999, it's 500 years into the future and pandemonium has broken out. Micro mini skirted news reporter Ulala is out to scoop the story while saving Earth from the Morolians who are forcing the citizens to dance against their will. By copying the dance moves of her loathsome opponents, she defeats them one by one and moves onto the next level. Michael had heard about *SC5* while it was still in its development phase and expressed interest in being involved. However, the game was almost completed at that point and it was only possible for him to have a brief cameo as the silver jumpsuited Space Michael. But when it came time for a sequel -- *Space Channel 5: Part 2* -- he was more fully-involved and received a much bigger part. Many of his celebrated moves were integrated into the dance sequences as well.

For years, rumours swirled throughout the gaming community that Michael had a hand in scoring music for Sega's *Sonic the Hedgehog* 3 (1994). After Michael's death, the speculation was confirmed true by one of his long-time collaborators, musician and arranger Brad Buxer, whom Michael called in to help with the project. Michael's name does not appear in the credits (though Brad's does) and it's unclear as to why he was never formally acknowledged for his work. Brad suggested that MJ wasn't happy with the game's sound quality and didn't want his name on the package while former Sega exec Roger Hector admitted the company tried to distance itself from Michael after allegations of child abuse were made public. Whatever the case, Brad did concede a long-standing belief that the music heard during the end credits later became the melody for "Stranger In Moscow".

Knowing of Michael's inclination to seek out new ways to showcase his music, John Branca and John McClain, co-executors of his estate, had been looking for the perfect company to develop an MJ dance game. In 2009, they approached Ubisoft, the software publisher behind the mega-hit, *Just Dance*. According to a press representative, the main objective was to "incorporate Michael's music and dance moves with the most innovative technology available." (usatoday 8/24/10) Hitting store shelves the following year, the interactive *Michael Jackson: The Experience* allows players to step into MJ's magical black penny loafers and (try to) replicate the choreography from some of his biggest hits and videos. No doubt, Michael would have loved it.

Opposite: Michael was a big collector of video games and pinball machines, many of which were part of a 2009 auction that was cancelled at the last minute.
Above: Michael visiting Sega Headquarters in Japan, with Sonic the Hedgehog.
Right: Television dancer Karina Smirnoff poses with a copy of the *Michael Jackson Experience* game upon its release in 2010.

BACK IN THE SWING OF THINGS

Four years had passed before any freshly baked Michael Jackson music was ready for delivery and as such, the anticipation built during the hiatus was as great as it had been for *Thriller* and *Bad*. But Top 40 radio had changed since 1987. Hip-hop culture had grown up and blown up; no longer just a "music fad", it had become a legitimate pop culture force, breaking out of boom boxes and right into film, television, fashion, and dance. Movies like *Boyz 'N The Hood, Do The Right Thing* and *House Party*, all set against hip-hop soundtracks, were racking up critical kudos and impressive box office returns. *In Living Color* and *The Fresh Prince Of Bel Air* ruled network TV with wicked humour and hip cast members that would go on to own Hollywood. In barber shops across America, young men were clipping their hair into hi-top fades and pairing their Chicago Bulls jerseys with day-glo togs from multi-culti clothing label Cross Colours. "Hip Hop Aerobics" classes even began popping up at fitness clubs when the dance moves that percolated from MTV became too widespread to ignore.

None of this was lost on Michael, who liked the new music he was hearing and hungered for a similar, more contemporary "urban" sound. He parted ways with Quincy Jones and teamed up with 23-year-old New Jack Swing kingpin Teddy Riley. An off-shoot of hip-hop, New Jack Swing fused the electronic dance beats of rap with the smooth vocal harmonies of R&B, becoming the preeminent clubland sound of the late eighties and early nineties. Teddy was already credited with pioneering the genre, producing Bobby Brown's 'My Prerogative', Keith Sweat's 'I Want Her' and 'Just Got Paid' by Johnny Kemp. By 1990, he was one of the most in-demand producers in the business and consequently just the man Michael wanted to help him stay current.

In 1993, Michael opened up to Oprah Winfrey for a live, 90-minute television interview which was watched by 90 million people. She later admitted, "After this interview, I thought I could be his friend, because I felt that he was really honest."

DANGEROUS

The fruit of the Riley/Jackson collaboration was *Dangerous*, which officially dropped in November, 1991. It was the first of Michael's albums to be formatted specifically for compact disc, a factor he took advantage of with a sprawling 77-minute, 14-song playlist. The title is yet another reference to Fred Astaire in *The Band Wagon*; "The girl was bad, the girl was dangerous" is not only a lyric from the 'Dangerous' track, but also a slightly altered version of a quote from Astaire in the film. As with all of Michael's prior albums, the groove was of utmost importance and *Dangerous* delivers its share of boogie down jams, albeit in an entirely new mode that favoured synthesized arrangements and machine-made samples. Rappers Heavy D and L.T.B. made cameos on *Dangerous*, in which half the album focused on love and heartbreak ('In The Closet', 'Give Into Me' and 'Who Is It?'). The remainder was heavy on socially conscious messages, reflecting on race relations ('Black Or White'), global poverty ('Heal The World') and the AIDS epidemic ('Gone Too Soon', dedicated to American teenager and AIDS activist Ryan White).

A PAIR OF EYES

Also changed up from past releases was the cover. Instead of a photograph of Michael, *Dangerous* featured a curious, surreal illustration by painter Mark Ryden. With its swirling storybook pastiche derived from 19th century circus posters, it quickly recalls the artwork for the Beatles' masterpiece, *Sgt. Pepper's Lonely Hearts Club Band*. The carnival of demented amusement rides from the 'Leave Me Alone' film was Ryden's jumping off point, with Michael suggesting specific facets of his legacy he wanted to include. The singer appears only as a pair of eyes watching over the fun park, peering out from behind a theatrical mask with his name emblazoned across the forehead in marquee lights. The assemblage of conflicting images included a half white and half black statue bust of a boy, a peacock sitting front and centre, and young Michael sharing a Pirates Of The Caribbean-style boat ride with Macaulay Culkin and Bubbles the chimp. Fans began to dissect the artwork, squinting at it, picking out every symbol and attempting to interpret what they meant. What was MJ alluding to with animal skeletons and skull and crossbones alongside cherubs and faeries? Were they cryptic messages sent to fans from their reclusive hero? To this day, some conspiracy theorists are convinced that "occult" symbols like the Eye of Providence and Twin Pillars indicate that Michael must have been a devil-worshipping member of the secret Illuminati society (as evidence, they also point to the portrait of circus master P.T. Barnum, whom they mistakenly identify as mystic figurehead Aleister Crowley). But in reality, Michael just wanted a mysterious cover for people to interpret however they wished.

Opposite: The curious *Dangerous* cover artwork led many fans to dissect the meaning in each alleged "symbol".
Above left: Teddy Riley was one of the hottest record producers of the 1990s.
Above right: Michael's all studded up, accepting the Good Scout Humanitarian Award in 1990.

> It was the first of Michael's albums to be formatted specifically for compact disc, a factor he took advantage of with a sprawling 77-minute, 14-song playlist.

DANGEROUS TERRITORY

'Black Or White' was chosen as *Dangerous*' lead single and its video was unveiled in similar fashion to 'Thriller' back in 1983. The debut was intended to be an event; a fire-engulfed television spot directed by David Lynch ran for weeks as did talk of the video's utilisation of an expensive new computer effects technique called "morphing". On November 14, 1991, Fox, MTV and BET in America all simultaneously aired 'Black Or White' as did networks in 27 countries worldwide. The first run audience was estimated to have been 500,000,000 people.

BLACK OR WHITE

The video reunited Michael with director John Landis and co-starred actors George Wendt, Tess Harper and Macaulay Culkin in an opening scene which cast Culkin as a bratty child who antagonises his father (Wendt) by playing his music way too loud. With one shred of an electric guitar, Culkin launches his father clear across the globe, landing him in the middle of the African wilderness where Michael is leading a group of dancing tribesmen. The bulk of 'Black Or White' features a string of similar vignettes placing Michael within a myriad of global backdrops: he sings alongside a group of classically trained Thai dancers; he joins a mini pow-wow with headress-wearing Native Americans. After dueting with a Bharata Natyam-dancing woman from India, he lands in a snowy Slavic village, surrounded by a circle of men demonstrating traditional Russian folklore-style footwork. The representatives of each country are decked out in full national regalia while Michael's own ensemble is a blank canvas consisting of a white shirt and tee, black pants, and loafers. Costume designer Deborah Nadoolman Landis, who purposely pared down Michael's outfit to offset the lush scenery and well-dressed dancers, described the ensemble as "pure Astaire" and went on to add, "I pushed him to lose the baroque gold braid of his personal wardrobe and get modern with his dance clothes and he responded happily." Vincent Paterson choreographed the vid, where Michael learned

snippets of the traditional dances from each destination and seamlessly mixed them with his own shoulder jerks and head pops.

The video concluded with the much talked about "morphing" segment, wherein a series of male and female faces of different ethnicities fluidly transform into one another while mouthing "It's black, it's white". The overall effect is a live-action version of a United Colours of Benetton print ad. At the time, feature-based image metamorphosis was a relatively new technology that cost thousands of dollars per minute to render but Michael, as always, wanted to top himself and please his fans which ultimately meant that price was of no concern.

BLACK PANTHER

Following the playful multi-culti morphing bit was a strange four and a half minute finale in which, after a black panther morphs into Michael, the singer became uncharacteristically aggressive, dancing in an incredibly angry nature, grabbing his crotch and grinding incessantly. He jumped atop cars and smashed windows while wielding a crowbar. There is no music or dialogue, just the frustrated sounds of Michael's shuffling feet, finger snaps, heavy breathing, and the shattering of glass.

According to Michael, the panther symbolised his animal instincts while the property destruction suggested how he wanted to annihilate racism. Viewers, "offended" by the violence and the sexually charged choreography, called up the networks and voiced their complaints. Within 48 hours, those final four minutes were quietly lopped off for future airings, an action which was accompanied by an apologetic statement from Michael, stating, "It upsets me to think that 'Black Or White' could have influenced any child or adult to destructive behaviour... I've always tried to be a good role model and, therefore, have made these changes to avoid any possibility of adversely affecting any individual's behaviour."

ILLUSION

Perhaps as a response to all of the negative publicity surrounding 'Black Or White', Michael switched gears entirely with his next video, 'Remember The Time'. John Singleton of *Boyz 'N The Hood* directed the peppy rom-com caper set within a lavish gold-encrusted ancient Egyptian kingdom. Supermodel Iman and actor Eddie Murphy played opposite each other as the perennially jaded Queen Nefertiti and her tightly wound Pharaoh, Ramses II, with basketball legend Earvin "Magic" Johnson as their trusty palace guard. Michael is an illusionist, the only performer in the entire kingdom who can successfully cure the Queen's chronic boredom. After seeing his act, she promptly falls in love with him, much to the dismay of her Pharaoh who spends the rest of the video trying to eliminate the competition. Michael, chased by an army of bare-chested thugs, is decked out in fancy, if somewhat confusing, accoutrements — a ceremonial kilt and wing-shaped metal chest plate with heavy black trousers and long-sleeve gold turtleneck, puzzling choices for a story set in sweltering Egypt. The Queen doesn't seem to notice though because when she finally gets her man, she plants a big ol' G-rated kiss right on him.

EGYPT

'Remember The Time' is visually reminiscent of biblical Hollywood sagas like *Cleopatra* and *The Ten Commandments* and though the cost of Michael's Egyptian mini-epic was undisclosed, it could easily have been just as pricey. But Elizabeth Taylor and Charlton Heston never enjoyed the advantages of the special effects Michael made use of as he frequently vanished and materialised in a cloud of computer-generated pixie dust. When MJ first began throwing around ideas for the short film with John Singleton, the director was excited but told Michael that he'd only do the video if they cast only black people, to which Michael replied, "No problem". What Singleton had in mind for the big dance number was a hip hop flavoured "Egyptian Busby Berkeley sequence". Keen for Michael to learn some new moves, he put the choreography into the hands of 20-year-old Fatima Robinson, hired specifically for her expertise in hip hop. Dubbing her style "techno pop", she combined street jazz, roboting and King Tut hand gestures. It was Michael's first time attempting hip hop and like every new dance style that was introduced to him, he practised every slide, every turn, every gesture for hours on end, until he was a master.

Opposite: Michael kicks his heels up with a group of African tribesmen in 'Black Or White'.
Right: Michael backstage at the 1993 Soul Train Awards, wearing his 'Remember The Time' costume.

When Michael Jackson toured in 1992 and 1993 in support of his *Dangerous* album, he performed all over the world but he did not schedule any dates in his home country. However, he did make one solitary performance – at the Rose Bowl in Pasadena, California – and though it wasn't technically a tour stop, it turned out to be as historic as any of his other performances and yet another game-changing moment in the business of entertainment.

In the summer of 1992, Superbowl XXVII was in the planning stage when the National Football League and Radio City Music Hall (producers of the live musical portion of the event) collectively agreed they had to step it up big time when it came to organising a memorable half-time show. Up until then, half-time shows were akin to Amateur Hour; marching bands, Disney mascots, and the odd Olympic figure skater were pretty standard fare. In 1991, ratings had taken a significant dip during the segment after being outwitted by the programme *In Living Color* which was aired live on a competing television network at the same time. Determined to never let that happen again, Jim Steeg, the NFL's special events director, wanted to book a performer who would appeal to the 18-34 year-old male demographic and decided Michael Jackson was the right man for the job. MJ's manager at the time, Sandy Gallin, turned down the offer three times before an agreement was reached. Michael himself knew little about American football but they sold him on the idea after explaining how the Superbowl would be broadcast in over 100 nations, including Third-World countries and military bases that he would never get to visit on tour. It was a gamble for everyone involved but it was one that paid off immensely.

The show opened with two Michael Jackson body doubles popping up atop giant screens at opposite ends of Rose Bowl Stadium. Amid cannons shooting gold fireworks that matched the colour of his bandoleers, the real Michael was catapulted onto the main stage from a trap door underfoot. He ran through a medley of classics ('Jam', 'Billie Jean', 'Black Or White', 'We Are The World') before launching into his current hit at the time, 'Heal The World' where he was accompanied on stage by a 3,500 member children's choir. Mission was more than accomplished when the ratings were tallied: more people tuned in to catch the half-time show than had been watching the first two quarters of the game. The Dallas Cowboys must have been enjoying the production too as they went on to trounce the competition that day, beating the Buffalo Bills 52-17.

Despite not being schooled on the rules of most professional sports, Michael did know of the importance they held in the realm of popular culture. He was particularly baseball-friendly, befriending the greats of the game and whisking them into his own hemisphere where they were more than happy to play along. Former L.A. Laker Earvin "Magic" Johnson co-starred in the 'Remember The Time' film wearing a jeweled collar, gold kilt and not much else. This was followed by 'Jam' in which Michael teamed up with Chicago Bulls hoop-master Michael Jordan for an MJx2 b-ball pick-up game/dance-off (a basketball signed by both men was auctioned off in 2010 to the tune of $294,000). Shaquille O'Neal, who was testing out his hip hop chops, rapped on the *HIStory* track '2 Bad'. Kobe Bryant, another Laker, looked up to Michael as a friend and mentor, someone who turned him onto the work of Audrey Hepburn and Fred Astaire. Michael would explain how he mentally prepared for concerts and the process that went into making an album. "It was all the validation that I needed,"

Bryant reminisced in 2009, "to know that I had to focus on my craft and never waver."

An inspiration off the court for many athletes besides Bryant, his creativity also seeped into the locker rooms and out onto the playing field. One particularly successful story recounts how the 1983 Philadelphia 76ers basketball team replayed Michael's mythical *Motown 25* television performance as part of a pre-game routine and won the national championship a month later. 'Can Your Feel It?' from *Triumph* may not have charted particularly upon its release in 1980 but it went on to become a standard in the repertoire of many university marching bands – the dynamic intro and thundering orchestrations make for a rousing football halftime show. On several occasions, NFL quarterback Donovan McNabb performed the Moonwalk or the 'Thriller' dance during end zone touchdown celebrations.

After Michael's death, professional athletes were some of the first to pay tribute. Baseball players like Jimmy Rollins of the Philadelphia Phillies and the Seattle Mariners' Ken Griffey, Jr. both used MJ tunes for their at-bat music; Griffey even wore a single batting glove when he took his swings. Basketball star Ron Artest, who signed a $33 million deal with the Lakers only weeks after Michael's passing, chose to wear #37 on the back of his jersey, a nod to the number of weeks *Thriller* spent at number one. And over in football/ soccer, there's Englishman Bas Savage and American Clint Mathis, both of whom have spiced up post-goal celebrations with a little bit of Moonwalk action to varying degrees of accuracy. Kei Kamara went a bit further after scoring for the MLS Houston Dynamo: sprinting to a spot mid-field, he pulled a white glove from his pocket, slipped it on, and struck a couple of trademark MJ poses.

Opposite: LA Laker Elgin Baylor presents the J5 with a basketball to celebrate their Forum concert in 1970. **This page (clockwise):** The Atlanta Hawks' Harry the Hawk moonwalks at an NBA playoff game in 2010; Michael's red shirt and basketball from the 'Jam' video; the Phillie Phanatic, mascot for the Philadelphia Phillies, dances with a fan dressed as MJ at a 2009 World Series game; the Los Angeles Sol women's soccer team honours Michael's memory; Michael with NFL President Neil Austrian, receiving his official jacket at Superbowl XXVII Media Day in 1993.

THE SIMPLE LIFE

By the early nineties, the entertainment industry was in the midst of a serious downsizing. Splashy displays of ostentation were becoming increasingly passé as a period of minimalism and austerity was ushered in. Gangsta rap was growing in prominence, overshadowing the colourful, playful, party side of hip hop. On the rock'n'roll end of the music spectrum, kids traded in neon spandex and big hair for flannel shirts and tattered jeans dug up at local Goodwill stores. But perhaps one of the most glaring indications that a new guard was marching in was when Nirvana's breakthrough album *Nevermind* bumped Michael's *Dangerous* out of the number one spot atop the *Billboard* album chart, dragging in with it the age of grunge.

'REMEMBER THE TIME'

The film for 'Remember The Time', which was released only weeks after Nirvana conquered *Billboard*, was one of the first casualties in this sober new era and its lavishness quickly seemed terribly outdated. As a result, it marked one of the last instances in which Michael indulged in the gilded video excesses which fans had grown accustomed to. Moving forward, there was an obvious change of direction in his style, which became more reserved, on and off screen.

HERB RITTS

'In The Closet' was the third release from *Dangerous* and its video was undoubtedly a departure for Michael. The festivities were surprisingly scaled down: there was no mass ensemble dance routine, complicated scenery, computerised special effects, or elaborate costumes. Shot entirely in sepia tones in a southern California desert, it was even devoid of much colour. Michael teamed up with director Herb Ritts who, up until the late eighties, had spent his career photographing high fashion editorials and celebrity portraits for magazines like *Vogue*, *Vanity Fair* and *Elle*. He had only begun working in the music video medium several years earlier, collaborating with Madonna for the cover of her *True Blue* album. He subsequently shot her video for 'Cherish' in 1989, which raised his visibility and led to other sexy MTV delights including 'Wicked Game' by Chris Isaak and 'Love Will Never Do (Without You)' for Michael's sister Janet. Ritts' photographic mode was sultry and unfussy with clean lines and stark shadows, characteristics he easily shifted from the glossy pages to the television screen. He worked almost exclusively in black and white and had a thing for pairing video stars with his fashion model friends: 'Wicked Game' featured Helena Christensen, Janet cavorted with male mannequins Antonio Sabato Jr. and Djimon Hounsou in 'Love Will Never Do' and in Herb's clip for Jon Bon Jovi ('Please Come Home For Christmas'), Cindy Crawford co-starred.

Ritts stayed true to his proven formula for 'In The Closet' and coupled Michael with supermodel Naomi Campbell, setting them within the ruins

of a dusty Spanish village. Michael wore fewer articles of clothing than he had before, donning only a dirty white undershirt and high-waisted black pants. (Not to be outdone, Naomi's teeny tiny mini skirt and midriff-baring top took up even less space.) The two engage in a

"courtship dance"; as Naomi tries to seduce Michael with her endless hip gyrations, he counteracts with his own spicy Paso Doble moves. As Ritts explained in a 1992 interview, "It's really not about outrageous sets and 50 dancers this time. It's really about bringing Michael's energy out in a new way."

Fashion photographer Herb Ritts directed the 'In The Closet' video and shot these high-fashion promotional images in which Michael was dressed by Gianni Versace.

ROAD WARRIOR

The hoopla might have been minimised for 'In The Closet', but Michael had no intention of scaling down anything when it came to going back out on the road. The *Dangerous* world tour began in the summer of 1992, touching down first at the Olympic Stadium in Munich, Germany. It was evident from the start that Michael was bent on outdoing everything that he had accomplished with the *Bad* concerts of 1987-89.

There was so much equipment, over 100 tons, that two Boeing 747 jets and a fleet of trucks were required to transport the show from venue to venue. Michael Bush and Dennis Tompkins were paid $1,000,000 to create the massive wardrobe for Michael and crew, which included nearly 300 garments. Two costumes weighed in at 40 lbs each and reached nine-feet in height, festooned with 36,000 fibre optics sewn throughout which were operated by remote control. Another coat was rigged with reflecting tape and three dozen strobe lights requiring 3,000 volts of electricity which were conducted via a concealed battery. Michael's military fetish evolved this time into a series of cyber cop

uniforms, black and gold and holographic silver, which were decorated with criss-crossing bandoleers. He removed the jacket to reveal a tight gold fencing shirt which snapped at the crotch, a design inspired by a Gianni Versace outfit he had worn in a photo shoot. Wearing the bodysuit with black pants, the look was the menswear equivalent of the bustier and trouser ensemble Madonna filled out during her Blonde Ambition tour. Michael opened the show by springing vertically through a trap door in the stage amid a spray of gold pyro and smoke bombs, a move humorously called "The Toaster Entrance". Each night ended with yet another illusion, this time orchestrated by magician David Copperfield, in which Michael, dressed in full-on astronaut garb, strapped on a rocket pack and jetted straight up out of the stadium.

Opposite: Holographic biker jackets were part of Michael's wardrobe during the *Dangerous* tour.
Above: Guns N' Roses guitarist Slash makes a cameo appearance at one of the Japan dates on the tour. He also played on the *Dangerous* track 'Give In To Me'.

> **Michael Bush and Dennis Tompkins were paid $1,000,000 to create the massive wardrobe for Michael and crew, which included nearly 300 garments.**

DANGEROUS ON STAGE

In between the toaster and the rocket man was a concert comprised mostly of numbers which echoed the template from the *Bad* tour — wearing the clothing and working the choreography that had been seen in the videos — though the staging, costumes and the special effects had become more elaborate. However, for 'Smooth Criminal', Michael managed to replicate the anti-gravity lean that was accomplished in the video only with the aid of camera cuts and invisible wires. This time, innovation and function came into play in the form of specially designed shoes and pegs which were set in the stage floor. As the lights went down mid-song, a solo dancer drew attention centre stage under a single spotlight. Michael and gang shuffled off into the shadows and stepped onto the special fasteners which latched into the heels of their shoes. When ready, the lights went back on as the entire dance crew leaned forward 33 degrees, flawlessly executing that magical manouevre. So ingenious was the shoe design that Michael and his designers, who collaborated with him on the fantastic footwear, filed for a US patent in 1992. So now, not only was Michael a singer, dancer, composer, writer, and producer, but he could officially add "inventor" to that long list of professional titles.

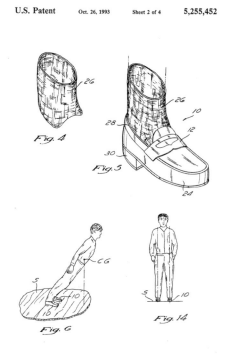

U.S. Patent   Oct. 26, 1993   Sheet 2 of 4   5,255,452

Centre: A copy of the US patent for the shoes that helped Michael and his dancers recreate the 'Smooth Criminal' lean during concert performances.
All other photos: Michael's costumes for the *Dangerous* world tour were more elaborate than those for previous tours.

Taking it to THE MAX

HEY, LITTLE SISTER

'In The Closet' was just the beginning of a new scaled-down version of Michael Jackson as his short films and overall artistic style became less opulent and more introspective, a trend that carried on through the remaining videos from *Dangerous* and right on over to 1995's *HIStory: Past, Present And Future, Book I*. Clips like those for 'Heal The World' and 'Gone Too Soon' were comprised almost entirely of newsreel snippets. The apocalyptic vision of 'Earth Song' was conveyed through a mix of documentary footage and original imagery shot in four different countries as Michael pleads for environmental sensitivity and an end to animal cruelty. 'Give In To Me', 'Who Is It?' and 'Stranger In Moscow' were more story-driven, with unknown actors playing bigger parts than Michael. One of the few playful videos during this period was 'Jam' where Michael matches wits (if not exactly hoop skills) with basketball legend Michael Jordan as the two meet up in a gritty old warehouse for a game of pick-up wearing off-the-rack red and black sportswear, the preferred colours of both the singer and the Chicago Bulls. However, amongst the series of message videos and moody narratives that were churned out during this period was one short film that, just like in the early days, changed the way MTV looked and sounded at a time when critics wondered if Michael had any relevance left in him. He was about to prove them wrong, and he brought his sister along with him for the ride.

JANET

There is no denying that of all the Jackson siblings, the only one to ever rival Michael's showmanship and fame was little sister Janet. The closest of all the kids in the family, they prompted one another's creativity with their individual styles, music and professional accomplishments. Janet admitted that *Thriller* motivated her to forge ahead with her breakthrough hit album *Control* in 1986. Similarly, Michael's *Dangerous* seemed to be influenced by his sister's 1989 dance floor opera *Janet Jackson's Rhythm Nation 1814*, which blended socially conscious lyrics with funk, soul and New Jack beats. By the late eighties, Janet had taken to wearing military gear and hiring an army of tightly choreographed dancers to back her up in videos like 'Rhythm Nation'. Her 'Black Cat' clip lifted Michael's 'Dirty Diana' imagery, from the concert hall setting right down to the billowing unbuttoned white shirt, tight black pants and strappy leg gear. The key that dangled from Janet's single hoop earring, a trademark during the eighties, was a gift from Michael that had once belonged to one of the animal cages at the house in Encino.

The long dreamed of Jackson-Jackson duet finally came about in 1995. Michael was desperate to express his fury and exasperation following the negative press attention that came with the allegations of child molestation made against him in 1993. "He was very upset and very angry and he had so much pent up in him that he wanted to get out," Janet told MTV. Janet came to her big brother's aid and brought along her longtime producers Jimmy Jam and Terry Lewis. "I played the role that I've always played in his life: his little sister that was there by his side, that had his back no matter what." What the foursome came up with was 'Scream', a lyrical slam against the media that mashed in bits and pieces of techno, house and hip hop.

Opposite: Michael kisses Janet after she presented him with a Grammy Legend Award in 1993.
Above left: Janet's key earring was a gift from Michael.
Above right: Janet's white blouse/tight black pants combo was very similar to Michael's 'Dirty Diana' outfit.

'SCREAM'

The short film for 'Scream' was an exhilarating departure from the selection of gloomy doldrums that otherwise populated MTV in the mid-nineties. Visionary Mark Romanek directed the $7 million video, an interstellar fantasy piece that mixed campy B-movie sci-fi with Japanese animation. Shot entirely in slick black and white, Michael and Janet are shown living together on a spacecraft, bouncing through the multi-room vehicle, behaving like siblings on a weekend joyride after stealing mom and dad's car. But these are not two rebellious teenagers having fun as claustrophobia and feelings of being caged in arise. Dressed in white like a strait-jacketed mental patient, Janet pounds her fists against the white walls of a padded cell. Michael smashes a series of V-neck guitars and dizzyingly spins like a pinwheel in mid-air, a wink at Alfred Hitchcock's *Vertigo*. Before long, the starship becomes a metaphor for the vacuum that Michael's life had become. Michael and Janet have undeniable chemistry as they play on like a couple of bratty kids, fighting over the video game controller and flipping off the camera, all of which is capped off by a Jackson vs. Jackson dance-off. It's a singular moment in music video history and watching the differing styles of the siblings is joyful; while Michael is very poised and technically precise, Janet thrashes and stomps, adding a bit of street cred to the proceedings.

'EDWARD SCISSORHANDS MEETS FUTURISTIC JAPANESE SUPERHERO'

Art director Tom Foden's expansive retro modernist playground (10 sets in all were built for the video) works as an exaggerated re-imagining of the stark, minimal decor from Stanley Kubrick's *2001: A Space Odyssey*.

Conversely, Michael and Janet's appearance is anything but throwback and draws heavily upon the industrial styles of nineties superstars Marilyn Manson and Trent Reznor of Nine Inch Nails, whose 'Closer' vid was also directed by Romanek. Janet is transformed into a ferocious, formidable vixen rocking an unkempt nest of hair, heavily smoked out eyes and black fingernails, a look her make-up artist Kevyn Aucoin described as 'Edward Scissorhands-meets-futuristic Japanese superhero'. Michael is an otherworldly android, with his gangly figure, ghostly complexion and long stringy jet black curls. They both run through a series of costume changes consisting of metallic spandex — bikini for her, jumpsuit for him — latex pants, shaggy coats and moon crater sweaters, all dreamed up by Michael's costumers Tompkins and Bush. "The clip's great allure is that neither of the siblings looks quite real," proclaimed the *New York Daily News* of the duo's fearsome, fashion-forward art-house glam.

'Scream' won three MTV Video Music Awards and a Grammy for "Best Music Video, Short Form". It was also part of a wave of imaginative new videos that changed the tide of what was being seen on music television; after years of frugality, record companies started opening up their wallets once again, investing more in promo clips than they had in half a decade. 'Scream' became wildly influential, its essence captured in countless videos for years to come. The ultramodern sets, austere lighting and fish eye lens camera shots can be seen in Jamiroquai's 'Virtual Insanity', 'The Universal' by Blur, and N'Sync's 'Bye Bye Bye'. Particularly taken with this approach to music video-making was director Hype Williams, whose entire late nineties reel of work, which includes TLC's 'No Scrubs' and Missy Elliott's 'She's A Bitch', is littered with spawns of 'Scream'.

Above: Michael and Janet sharing a zen moment in the 'Scream' video.
Opposite: Michael's silver costume was the same one his 'Space Michael' character wore in the video game, *Space Channel 5*.

HISTORY IN THE MAKING

Michael and Janet's us-against-the-world duet was the lead single released from Michael's *HIStory: Past, Present And Future, Book I*, a double disc package that included 15 digitally remastered 'greatest hits' tracks ('HIStory Begins'), fifteen new songs ('HIStory Continues), a lavish 52-page booklet, and a costly $32.98 price tag. The album included the first batch of new MJ material post-scandal, a fact that effactually made its performance closely watched and scrutinised by music industry insiders. 'Scream', which was dropped several weeks before *HIStory*, had performed fairly well, reaching the Top 5 in most countries. So both Michael and Sony (his current label after it had bought out CBS) held out hope that despite the recent years of brutally bad press, his sales numbers wouldn't be terribly affected. Nevertheless, they weren't about to take any chances and thus, *HIStory* was launched with a marketing campaign that would cost over $30 million and become one of the most expensive in the annals of popular music.

GOOSE-STEPPING

First up was the four-minute $4 million *HIStory* teaser commercial. Shot in Hungary, it co-starred a troop of bare-chested metalsmiths wielding large mallets among vats of melted steel and flying sparks. The scene

cut back-and-forth to Michael, decked out in his finest black and silver soldier finery and mirrored aviators, leading a goose-stepping Communist army through the streets of a Soviet Bloc city. Instead of a song from the album, Basil Poledouris' theme from the film *Hunt For Red October* was the soundtrack as the brigade turned into a ticker tape parade with fans lining the streets, screaming, crying and fainting as their 'hero' returns home from war (with the press, one can only assume). In the town square, helicopters circle overhead and searchlights scan the airspace while the sculptors' masterpiece is unveiled: a skyscraper-high statue of the King of Pop sporting the same severe militia garb as he had during the *Dangerous* tour.

Sony saturated the airwaves of MTV, BET and VH-1 with abbreviated versions of the spot while movie theatres showed the entire clip during feature film previews. A JumboTron was placed in New York City's Times Square with a clock that counted down the days to *HIStory*'s release.

Michael even agreed to a rare television interview on American TV where he and wife Lisa Marie Presley sat down to talk with journalist Diane Sawyer to an audience estimated at 60 million. However, this all paled in comparison to the enormous promotional push that was seen in Europe.

Above: Michael's teaser for *HIStory* featured him marching in a victory parade down the streets of Budapest.
Opposite above left: A billboard in Times Square, NYC.
Opposite above right: A scene from 'They Don't Care About Us' shot in Rio de Janeiro – a second video for this song showed Michael behind prison bars.
Opposite bottom: More Communist imagery, on the *HIStory* tour in 1996.

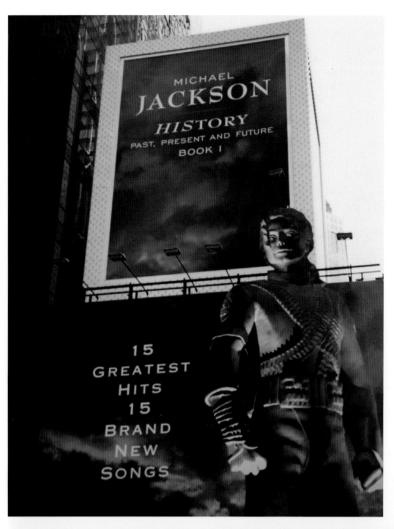

This page (clockwise): A series of photos and costumes from the *HIStory* world tour.
Opposite left: To promote *HIStory*, a barge with Michael's giant likeness was sent down the River Thames in London.
Opposite right: On the tour, Michael made his grand entrance to the stage via spaceship.

THE STATUE

Legend has it that when Sony approached Michael about marketing possibilities for *HIStory*, he responded, "Build a statue of me." Ask for it, and it shall come. Nine Michael Jackson statues were constructed, all identical to the one shown at the end of the commercial. English sculptor Derek Haworth designed the 32 foot well-dressed leviathans which were constructed of steel and fibreglass. They were then hauled off and erected in various European cities, including Berlin, Germany and Eindhoven, Netherlands. It was London, however, that saw the most extravagant unveiling of all: Michael's three-story likeness was towed down the River Thames by barge, a journey that meant Tower Bridge was raised to allow the mammoth metal pop star to sail by. Real live Michael Jackson look-alikes populated local record shops while six-foot tall cardboard replicas were also scattered in retail stores. Hardcore fans may have been in awe but media pundits were growing increasingly critical of what seemed to be a bad case of megalomania.

THE HISTORY CONTROVERSIES

As far as the actual new music was concerned, opinions varied as to whether *HIStory* lived up to the hype or not, but all agreed that it was Michael's anger and resentment towards the media that had fueled the tortured writing, with the *NY Times* calling it "a psychobiographer's playground". 'Scream' and 'Tabloid Junkie' both railed against the vindictive tendencies of the press, the orchestral ballad 'Have You Seen My Childhood?' begged the listener for a little sympathy and on 'Money', Michael sang about the lecherous hangers-on who tried to drain his bank account. Controversy erupted into 'Black Or White'-sized proportions with 'They Don't Care About Us' in which Michael used anti-Semitic-laden lyrics ('Jew me, sue me/Kick me, kike me') to convey how he felt he had been victimised. And then eyebrows were raised for entirely different reasons when he, and wife Lisa Marie, stripped down to near-nakedness in the video for 'You Are Not Alone'; when some of Michael's not-suitable-for-basic-cable body parts were exposed in one scene, they were eventually digitally covered by a white sheet. The inner book was peppered with photos of Michael at various points throughout his life and included testimonials from the celebrated members of his inner circle, including Jackie Kennedy Onassis, Steven Spielberg, and Elizabeth Taylor. (It was Taylor who first referred to her pal as 'The true King of Pop, Rock and Soul', giving Michael the royal title many thought he had anointed upon himself.) Also included were two works of art by Gottfried Helnwein, an Austrian painter/photographer whose signature depictions of troubled, wounded children were a perfect fit for Michael's current state of mind. Standing out, though, was a jarring pencil sketch of a toddler-aged child huddled in a corner clutching a microphone, a portrait rendered by Michael himself.

EVER MORE GRANDIOSE

For the *HIStory* tour that straddled 1996 and '97 Michael again built on the foundation of concert tours past and stuck closely to his audience-approved formula while making the festivities even more grandiose than ever. There were larger sets, more dancers, flashier costumes; even his 'freezes' (those moments where he just stood still like a statue, lingering as the audience got louder) seemed to last longer. Stepping out from an intergalactic time machine at the top of each show, he fashioned himself a robotic space cowboy, evoking both C-3PO and John Wayne in a western bib-front suit of gold and silver lamé complete with thigh-high 18-carat gold plated greaves and breastplate. Most of the drills were faithfully resurrected from the past, right down to the 'Smooth Criminal' suits, the disappearing magic act, and Michael's boom-lift entrance into 'Beat It' which had been part of the scheme since the *Bad* tour.

He did put a delightful new Chaplin-like whirl to 'Billie Jean', however, wobbling onto the stage in a plain T-shirt and black trousers, tattered old satchel in tow. He channelled the master comic by staying completely quiet, tilting his head, shrugging, sighing. But what was in the suitcase? After opening it, he pulled out one by one the now iconic items that he had been wearing for 'Billie Jean' ever since that Motown night in 1983: a black sequin jacket, white glove, black fedora. Each piece got closely inspected, and then tried on and tested out with a few shakes and poses. After tottering around the dark stage and circling the outer edge of the spotlight, he playfully scooted into the light and turned on the tune. It was a silent movie scene come to life in which Michael appeared on stage in absolute quietude for over three minutes, an eternity in a live concert setting, and practically unheard of in pop. Unless, of course, you are the King.

GHOSTS

Before heading out on the road to promote *HIStory*, Michael finally completed a project that had been on the back burner for over three years, *Michael Jackson's Ghosts*. Prepping for the mini flick began back in 1993 but production fell into an indeterminate state of limbo when Michael found himself in the middle of the scandal. When filming was scheduled to resume in the winter of 1995, proceedings were halted yet again when he wound up in the hospital while rehearsing for a television concert in NYC. By the time the movie was officially back on track, the director Mick Garris had to bow out due to professional conflicts. In to replace him was Stan Winston, who Michael had first met way back in 1977 when he designed Michael's Scarecrow make-up for *The Wiz*. Coincidentally, also blasting in from the seventies was costume designer Warden Neil, who had, along with Bill Whitten, designed wardrobe for *The Jacksons* variety show.

Like every new enterprise Michael took on, *Ghosts*, which initially went by the title *Is This Scary?*, took him on yet another journey in which he set out to transcend anything he had accomplished before – the special effects, computer graphics, make-up, and dance numbers needed to be grander and more technologically advanced than ever. Michael even pushed his acting abilities to the limits when Winston suggested that he play multiple roles, a dare he wasn't about to walk away from. He enjoyed a good challenge as well as the extra long sessions in the make-up chair that came with it.

MAESTRO

The central character he portrays is the eccentric Maestro, a pallid oddball of a guy who dresses in frilly 18th century finery and lives inside a misty hilltop estate on the outskirts of a town called Normal Valley. He gets a kick out of entertaining the neighbourhood kids with a few magic tricks and some good-natured scares but once the parents learn of the wacky dude, they set out on an old-fashioned witch-hunt led by the town's Mayor, a middle-aged, heavy set white man also played by Michael. With torches in hand, they converge on the dusty lair where they are confronted by Maestro who tries to convince them that while he may be different, he is not a bad guy. "You're weird, you're strange and I don't like you," spits the Mayor. Maestro, who grows increasingly aggravated, takes matters into his own hands, inviting his fellow ghosts out of hiding to join him for what he knows will be a crowd-pleasing supernatural dance party. But while the kids and their parents begin to

loosen up, the Mayor is not impressed. It is then that the exasperated Maestro turns into 'ectoplasmic sludge' and possesses the villain's body, leading to a nutty dance sequence of the balding 50-something Moonwalking, popping and grabbing his crotch. Ultimately, the Maestro wins over the haters and the Mayor runs off scared to tears.

STEPHEN KING

Although *Ghosts* was co-written by best-selling novelist Stephen King, the horror-musical has a decidedly Tim Burton feel, from the rubbery facial expressions and pop-out eyeballs of the *Beetlejuice* variety to the Danny Elfman-soundalike score (indeed, MJ was a huge Burton fan and even lobbied to play the title role in *Edward Scissorhands*, a part that ultimately went to Johnny Depp). Michael performs three songs during the 38-minute piece, '2-Bad', 'Is It Scary' and 'Ghost', the latter two being new songs which were part of the 1997 album, *Blood On The Dance Floor: HIStory In The Mix*. And while the acting is frequently mediocre – save for an early comedic performance from rapper/actor Mos Def – the dance numbers come to the rescue. They are the highlight of the movie, as Michael leads his very own paranormal coterie through some superb Travis Payne/LaVelle Smith choreography that was even more impressive once the special effects and fancy editing came into play. Ghouls march up and down walls, across the ceiling and through pillars as Michael peels off his flesh suit, his skeleton emerging to entertain the crowd.

Although *Ghosts* was an incredibly ambitious endeavour, it never saw the inside of American movie houses. It was featured in a special midnight screening at the Cannes Film Festival in 1997 and played alongside *Stephen King's Thinner* in a handful of European cinemas. It was released internationally on VHS cassette and was later refashioned into a special that aired on VH-1 as part of a Michael Jackson Halloween spectacular in the early 2000s.

This page: Several of the masks used in Ghosts (top) and an official movie poster (above).
Opposite: Michael as the Maestro.

DESIGN OF THE TIMES

For the last 25 years of Michael Jackson's life, Michael Bush and Dennis Tompkins were his on-call costumers. The relationship began on the set of *Captain EO* when Bush was assisting another designer and struck up a friendship with the film's star. A native of Sciotoville, Ohio, Bush began his working life as a floral designer, a career that led him to Las Vegas where he managed a flower shop at the MGM Grand. Shortly thereafter, he moved even further west, landing in Los Angeles where, while making ends meet as a Universal Studios tour guide, he met future business partner, costume designer Dennis Tompkins. Bush, who had been sewing since he was a teenager, quickly switched professions and the pair went on to design clothes for soapy television programmes including *The Young And The Restless*, *General Hospital* and *Dynasty*. But once they hooked up with the biggest pop star on the planet, their focus shifted completely. "He's kept us almost exclusive by keeping us so busy," Bush said in a 1992 interview.

Busy was putting it mildly. Nearly every time MJ appeared in public, whether it was an awards show, Pepsi commercial, or Elizabeth Taylor wedding, he was wearing a Tompkins Bush original. Their Los Feliz studio employed nearly 60 stitchers, drapers and pattern makers, churning out all manner of fancy beaded military suits, holographic jackets and buckle-laden biker gear. Bush also went on the road with Michael, acting as his personal wardrobe master on tour while Tompkins stayed back in California running the shop. They even had a mannequin built to Michael's exact measurements.

The designers always kept a fairly low profile which meant very few people outside of the industry knew the names behind Michael's celebrated wardrobe. However, in the spring of 2005, their handiwork became increasingly scrutinised as cameras followed Michael on his daily walk into the Santa Monica Courthouse. Media coverage of his child abuse trial was overwhelming as hundreds of members of the worldwide press set up camp outside the building for 18 weeks while proceedings took place inside. It was one of the biggest reality shows ever, with news reporters, TV pundits, talking heads and body language experts all weighing in on their opinions as to what might be going on in Michael's head. With not much information to cast any accurate speculations, their eyes became increasingly focused on what he was wearing. Tompkins and Bush were behind every single look Michael wore throughout, a labour of love which turned into a daily ritual during the four and a half months he spent on trial. Bush's morning began with a pre-dawn wake-up call and two-hour drive out to Neverland Ranch where, at around 6am, he would present Michael with a crisp new outfit straight from the sewing room. After a quick hug and "thank you", the designer would be out the door, back to the studio to continue working on the next day's ensemble. Three tailors around Los Angeles helped knock out the jackets in quick succession due to the incredibly short turnover time.

The clothing was as thoughtfully crafted as the wardrobe for any scripted film. It was a challenge for the designers to create outfits that were not only courtroom appropriate but would also showcase Michael in a positive light and let him be true to his own style. On the first day of the trial, he wore head-to-toe white, a symbol of purity and innocence. "We started with the white suit and everyone went crazy," Michael Bush recounted in May 2005. "So we went to dark suits — the navy blues, the blacks, grey pinstripes. Then we put the red double-breasted blazer on him — well, the world stopped."

The parade of regal, aristocratic uniforms turned Michael's painstaking walk from his black SUV to court house doors into a daily runway event for everyone else. There were frock coats, armbands, gold braiding, and a smattering of cavalry medals. Overall, the looks were quite elegant and dapper, with old-timey details like silk pocket squares and brocade vests. Never wearing the same ensemble twice, each day's furnishings were aimed to help raise the spirits of the crestfallen star and on more than one occasion, his family showed their love and support by coordinating their own outfits with his. On June 13, 2005, Michael was acquitted of all charges and wearing his most sober outfit of all, a fit black suit and skinny tie, he walked that imaginary red carpet for the very last time.

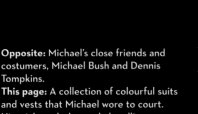

Opposite: Michael's close friends and costumers, Michael Bush and Dennis Tompkins.
This page: A collection of colourful suits and vests that Michael wore to court. His trial wardrobe made headline news.

FASHION, FORWARD

Michael had been keeping a relatively low profile in the decade following the *HIStory* tour, stepping out only under extraordinary circumstances. On September 7 and 10, 2001, he celebrated 30 years as a solo artist with a set of concerts held in his honour at Madison Square Garden in New York City ('Got To Be There', his debut solo outing, was released in 1971). The following month, he performed in Washington, DC for the 'United We Stand: What More Can I Give' benefit concert and tribute to the victims of the 9/11 tragedy. And a week later, his tenth studio album, *Invincible*, was released. After his 2005 trial and acquittal from charges of child abuse, he disappeared entirely, living in seclusion with his three children, spending time in Bahrain, France and Ireland. But on the eve of the quarter century anniversary of *Thriller* in 2007 and release of the *Thriller* 25 CD, Michael was ready to emerge from his hideout. So when it came time to reminisce about the Best Selling Album in the World, he granted several high profile publications more access than he had allowed in years and showed off the style idol side of himself that had been all but forgotten.

It took *Ebony* magazine's creative director Harriette Cole a year to secure Michael for his first post-trial interview, where he revealed how classical music was his true "first love" and that he saw himself being "more productive in film and directing" than on stage. Accompanying the article was a sumptuous fashion spread shot by photographer Matthew Rolston at the Beaux-Arts Court of the Brooklyn Museum, a monolithic locale chosen after Michael expressed a desire to be photographed amongst works of art. Stylist Phillip Bloch dressed the star in a series of swanky pieces from Hugo Boss, Emporio Armani and Yohji Yamamoto, a selection which MJ became so smitten with that he wanted to take it all home.

The image used for the cover, a portrait of Michael in a pristine white Valentino tuxedo, was chosen for its clean, iconic imagery and evoked the white Rick Pallack suit from the *Thriller* album. Also an eighties throwback were the oversized diamond brooches which recalled the antique jewellery Michael had worn in the best-selling yellow vest and bow tie poster, a shot Rolston had also taken. But as much as Michael enjoyed playing dress-up, Bloch would later admit, "Jackson wasn't up on pop culture or fashion." In fact, when Michael showed particular affection for a slim Burberry jacket adorned with epaulettes, he was surprised to learn from Bloch that military looks were especially popular, responding, "Really? That's in fashion now?"

"I DON'T CARE ABOUT EVERYDAY CLOTHES"

In the grand scheme of things, it's easy to understand why MJ, whose clothing choices were as lauded in the earlier years as they were dismissed later on, might not have been as well-schooled in the art of fashion as he was in the fine arts. Ever since the days at Motown when he and his brothers kicked it in kooky Boyd Clopton garb, Michael had almost exclusively been dressed by costumers, a practice similar to the old Hollywood tradition when film studio costume designers would also outfit their actresses off screen. Often asked about his thoughts on fashion, he conceded that being on-trend wasn't on the top of his list of priorities. "I don't care about everyday clothes," was a standard response. At one point during the *Bad*-era, Madonna, herself an avid student of designer labels, decided that Michael needed some help in the wardrobe department, humorously remarking, "I would like to completely redo his whole image... I want to get him out of those buckly boots and all that stuff."

Michael wasn't as stylistically clueless as Phillip Bloch or Madonna seemed to assume, however. Throughout the eighties and nineties, he had regularly tapped Gianni Versace for his fashion genius; the Italian's designs can be seen in a wide range of MJ projects from the screwball retro finery of the 'Say, Say, Say' video to the gold spandex bodysuit of the *Dangerous* tour. (Before his death in 1997, it had even been rumoured that Versace was in the midst of working on a $65,000 air-conditioned coat for Michael to wear on stage). In later years, the singer had grown close with "King of Bling" Roberto Cavalli who dressed him for several high profile events and was name-dropped as the designer for a proposed world tour in 2007 than never happened.

Nevertheless, entertainment culture had changed dramatically since the eighties and now celebrities were expected to know the difference between Lanvin and Louis Vuitton. Actresses and pop stars began to moonlight as fashion models, replacing them on the covers of glossy magazines and in the designer editorials that sprung from the pages. And it was this aspect of fashion that Michael wasn't terribly familiar with. While picture sessions had been common since the Jackson 5 days, he hadn't really done a proper fashion editorial before, the closest being a series of Herb Ritts promo photos for *Dangerous* where he wore head-to-toe Versace. But that all changed in the fall of 2007 when not only did he pose for *Ebony*, but also in the pages of one of the most respected publications in the fashion industry, *L'Uomo Vogue*.

VOGUE MODEL

Like *Ebony*, it was *Thriller*'s impending birthday that motivated *L'Uomo Vogue* fashion editor Rushka Bergman to approach Michael about being photographed. Much to her surprise, he liked the idea. Once she started contacting designers to pull looks for the shoot, it became clear that everybody wanted him to wear their clothes: 62 members of fashion's elite sent 300 looks and nearly 200 pairs of shoes for the King of Pop. The lengthy black and white spread, shot by Bruce Weber, boasted styles from Cavalli, Burberry and Dior Homme, a label renowned for its impossibly narrow, tailored silhouette that was favored by a younger generation of rock bands, including Green Day and Franz Ferdinand. *Uomo*'s cover photo, a modern-day *Off The Wall*, showed Michael, all smiles, wearing a trim Dior tuxedo, a perfect (if unintentional) set-up to *Ebony*'s *Thriller*-esque image, which was published two months later.

Once *L'Uomo Vogue* hit the newsstands in October, Weber's high-style images quickly spread across cyberspace, beguiling long-term MJ fans and label lovers alike, setting into motion Michael's latter-day status as a darling of the fashion industry. Helping him along the way was Bergman, who impressed Michael with her work ethic and meticulous taste in clothes. After *L'Uomo Vogue*, he brought the Serbian-born fashion editor into his circle to act as his personal stylist and creative consultant. The timing of this union was impeccable as there was already an eighties fashion revival in full swing on the designer catwalks and in style blogs, making the *Thriller* silhouette of skinny jeans and strong shoulders highly covetable. His sartorial transformation was closely monitored as Bergman's influence became more apparent.

A feverish pitch was reached in the spring of 2009 when paparazzi photos were published of Michael wearing a suit by Tom Ford atop a sparkling Balmain T-shirt that wasn't yet available for sale. Fashion bloggers watched as snapshots emerged almost daily of Michael wearing a series of pieces from the French design house, its jackets easily identifiable by their surrealistically peaked shoulders. Crafted by designer Christophe Decarnin, the Balmain aesthetic (which was often compared to that of Gianni Versace) was heavily influenced by eighties MTV, with several collections clearly inspired by Michael. Souped-up frogging and intricate bead work of Decarnin's spring 2009 military jackets became hallmarks of "Balmainia". The autumn 2009 runway show even opened with 'Don't Stop ('Til You Get Enough)' blasting from the speakers and featured models wearing black and silver togs swathed in Swarovski crystals, a combination which recalled Bill Whitten's designs of the *Off The Wall* period.

The idea of Michael wearing the Balmain threads which he had inspired left many in a frenzy. *Vogue Paris* Fashion Director Emmanuelle Alt was said to have been "obsessed" with Michael, verging on tears at the idea of him wearing Balmain on stage. He gained a whole new fanbase of young, rabid fashion fanatics who called the Jackson/Balmain pairing "revolutionary and iconic" and "ferocity at the highest level". Bergman had the keen eye to choose clothing for Michael that fit his personal style but was more current and directional. She adoringly referred to him as her "supermodel" because even at 5'10' tall, he could fit into a woman's size two and wear designer samples straight off the runway. No longer would Michael be the butt of jokes about an overabundance of belt buckles and never again did he wear pyjama bottoms out in public.

Opposite left: Michael wore a suit by Roberto Cavalli to the 2006 World Music Awards.
Opposite centre: Rocking a head-to-toe Givenchy in 2009.
Opposite right: Balmain's Spring 2009 collection was heavily influenced by Michael's style, especially this military jacket, which Michael himself wore.
Right: In this image from the *Ebony* shoot, Michael wears an ivory Valentino tuxedo and Lanvin shirt.

THE FINAL CURTAIN

As the 25th anniversary of *Thriller* approached, rumblings of a Michael Jackson comeback became louder and a residency in Las Vegas began to take shape. Hotel owners across The Strip boasted of contracts they were drawing up to lure the King to their court. "Leaked" to the press were preliminary sketches and concept art for the hullabaloo which showed futuristic, solar-powered costumes drawn up by fashion designer Andre Van Pier. Also proposed was a 50-foot tall statue of Michael to advertise the show; a gleaming, shining Jacksonian robot that would be seen as planes descended into the city's McCarran Airport. But while Michael was evaluating offers from various casino moguls, plans for a Vegas comeback were put on hold once he inked a deal to perform a series of gigs at London's O2 arena.

THE CANCELLED SHOWS

The concert dates, which had been speculated for months and two years in the planning, were announced by Michael himself to a screaming mob at a London press conference in March 2009. The show, entitled "This Is It", was to be Michael's curtain call, his final time performing in a live concert setting. Regardless of the fact that thousands of fans, many dressed in single gloves and black fedoras, turned up to witness the media event, industry insiders had their doubts, prompting such sentiments as, "Michael Jackson planning comeback in London but will anybody care?" Care they did, much to everyone's surprise, including

Michael himself. Fans queued up overnight in front of the O2 and heavy internet traffic crashed the ticket websites when dates went on sale the morning of March 13. The first batch of 10 shows quickly expanded into 50 when interest turned out to be "overwhelming". Over 800,000 seats were sold at a rate of 333 per minute in roughly five hours. It was estimated that the local economy would get a $500 million boost as a result of the residency.

As prepping and rehearsals for "This Is It" moved quickly forward in Los Angeles, the show took on a life of its own. Over 5,000 movers and shakers applied for the chance to fill 12 spots as Michael Jackson back-up dancers. The stage structure was the biggest ever built for an indoor arena with sets that rivalled those of the most elaborate Broadway musical, like a neon, seventies-style television variety show for the Motown medley and an expansive urban fire escape for 'The Way You Make Me Feel'. 'Thriller' and 'Earth Song' were backed by their own, original 3D special effects-laded short films. Pole dancers and aerialists added a Cirque du Soleil element as did the "grand illusions", orchestrated by magician Ed Alonzo (or David Copperfield or Criss Angel, depending on which newspaper was reporting). With costs estimated to have surpassed the $20 million mark, Randy Phillips, CEO of concert promoters AEG Live, described the production values as "the most cutting edge ever employed on a tour. We're using technology that's never been used before in live entertainment."

> **Over 800,000 seats were sold at a rate of 333 per minute in roughly five hours. It was estimated that the local economy would get a $500 million boost as a result of the residency.**

Above: Michael at a press conference to announce his 'This Is It' concert series in London.
Opposite top: Fans show off their tickets to one of the shows.
Opposite bottom: Michael and dancers rehearsing on the massive stage.

THIS IS IT

'This Is It''s creative team mixed old school with the new, beginning with familiar faces director/producer Kenny Ortega (*Dangerous* and *HIStory* tours) and choreographer/associated director Travis Payne ('Scream', *Ghosts*). Payne and Ortega organised a costume crew that not only brought back Michael Bush and Dennis Tompkins, but introduced a fresh face into the circle, Zaldy Goco. A young New York-based fashion designer well-known for his work with Gwen Stefani on her L.A.M.B. clothing label, Zaldy was chosen from a handful of hopefuls (including John Galliano and Alexander McQueen) whom Payne approached to submit costume ideas for consideration. "Zaldy is the new cool thing and working with him gave Michael credibility. But Michael Bush is near and dear to his heart. So I wanted them to collaborate," Payne later explained.

It was Zaldy who went on to become Michael's chief costumer, creating 10 of the 16 ensembles the star was to wear on stage. Although he was initially asked to "re-invent" MJ's stage persona, Zaldy instead chose to modernise the already existing catalogue of legendary looks explaining, "People were going to want to see those iconic images, made more relevant to the times. So, that's what my approach was — referencing what we knew, but bringing more technology and new techniques that Michael had never used before."

Over 300,000 Swarovski crystals were used to embellish the costumes, including the opening outfit, a futuristic space suit that was, as Zaldy described, "literally dipped in crystals". The complete look, which would be worn as Michael emerged from a nine-foot tall robot, also included matching sunglasses, shoes and skyscraper high Lucite shoulder pieces (at Michael's request, strong shoulders appeared throughout the wardrobe, the possible result of his newfound love of Balmain). The updated 'Thriller' jacket was cut from shiny red PVC and embroidered to look as though blood was dripping down from the shoulders. Zaldy mixed military styling and multi-ethnic arts for 'Heal The World' in which he built an eclectic high neck jacket that patched together traditional hand crafts from all of the globe, including beading from Africa, Chinese embroidery and Native American quilting. For 'Billie Jean', he stayed true to the original uniform but gave it cutting edge twist. Inspired by the light-up sidewalks of the short film, he worked with Philips Energy to turn the outfit into a one-man electrical parade, lighting up in a rainbow of colours, starting at the socks, running up the legs and arms, and then to that singular white glove. When Michael tried on the ensemble, he gasped and told the designer, "It's everything I always wanted!"

> **When Michael tried on the ensemble, he gasped and told the designer, "It's everything I always wanted!"**

The never-worn costumes from 'This Is It'.
Above: 'Heal The World' (left) and 'Man In The Mirror' (right).
Opposite: 'Wanna Be Startin' Something' (left), 'Thriller' (right) and the extensive shoe wardrobe, created by Christian Louboutin (bottom).

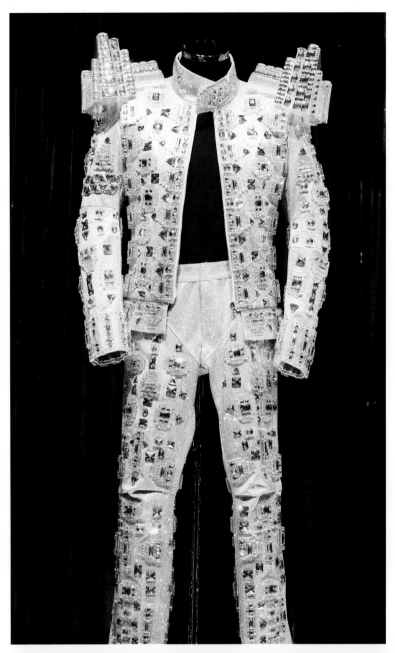

AND THE FANS PLAYED ON

The news of Michael Jackson's passing on June 25, 2009 was met with shock, disbelief and unprecedented worldwide sadness. The timing of his death only added to the sense of grief as the "This Is It" cast and crew were only a week away from flying to London to begin preparations for opening night. The internet nearly crashed as people scrambled to their keyboards to see if the news was true. Traffic on Twitter was so heavy — with over 5,000 Michael Jackson-related Tweets per minute — that many users were unable to log in to their accounts. Radio stations and music television channels immediately began

marathons of Michael's music and short films. On July 7, a memorial service at the Staples Center in Los Angeles drew an estimated one billion viewers worldwide when it was broadcast live on television and streamed via the internet. Sales of his music skyrocketed all over the planet, with his albums occupying multiple top spots on charts at iTunes, Amazon.com and in *Billboard* magazine where it was reported that over a million digital downloads of his recordings were sold in a single week, an achievement that had never been reached before by anyone. In a lot of ways, it was 1984 all over again.

It was reported that over a million digital downloads of his recordings were sold in a single week, an achievement that had never been reached before by anyone.

Above: A black fedora and white glove placed near Michael's name plaque on the Apollo Theater's Walk of Fame in NYC.
Opposite: A young fan mourns.

TRIBUTES

Madonna paid tribute during a concert at the O2 (just weeks before Michael was to take the stage), announcing, "Let's give it up to one of the greatest artists the world has ever known: Michael Jackson. Long live the king!" before introducing an MJ impersonator who busted out a few key dance moves during 'Wanna Be Startin' Somethin''. At a performance in Barcelona, Spain, Bono dedicated the U2 song 'Angel Of Harlem' to Michael and topped it off with a few bars of 'Man In The Mirror'. Even Prince, supposed rival of MJ during the eighties, covered 'Shake Your Body Down (To The Ground)' at several shows following Michael's passing. MTV honoured his career in spectacular fashion at the 2009 Video Music Awards with Michael's choreographers and dancers past and present, including Travis Payne, Tina Landon, Chris Judd, Wade Robson, and the cast of "This Is It". Dressed in 'Beat It' jackets and sequin military togs, they joined together in rhythmic harmony, smashing through a medley of Michael's biggest hits while his videos ran on a giant screen behind them. For the finale, Janet Jackson emerged for one more dance-off with her brother, dancing alongside his image during their one and only duet, 'Scream'.

But it was the millions of fans who showed an outpouring of love so far and wide and so heartfelt that it can only be described as unprecedented. Crowds gathered around Michael Jackson landmarks, his childhood home in Gary, Indiana, at the gates of Neverland Ranch, in a Regensdorf, Switzerland park where one of his *HIStory* statues was on display. Tribute events with DJs spinning non-stop Michael music popped up in hundreds of cities all over the world, from Beijing to Moscow, Mexico City to Melbourne, Tokyo to Brussels. At New York City's Apollo Theater, several thousand dedicated fans lined up in the pouring rain to attend a raucous memorial service of music and video footage led by film director Spike Lee who reminded the crowds, "It's all about the love."

And at each and every one of these events, dressed in black fedoras, shimmery gloves and mirrored aviator shades, fans literally danced in the streets, Moonwalking throughout a global dance party that lasted the rest of the summer. And as long as there is still Michael Jackson music in existence, it's a party that will likely never end.

> **But it was the millions of fans who showed an outpouring of love so far and wide and so heartfelt that it can only be described as unprecedented.**

Above: The stellar tribute at the 2009 MTV Video Music Awards featured Michael's dancer friends, as well as sister Janet.
Opposite left: A billboard announcing the release of the documentary film, *This is It*.
Opposite right: Madonna pays tribute with an MJ impersonator at a London date of her 'Sticky And Sweet Tour'.
Opposite bottom: Fans honour the life and legacy of their fallen idol.

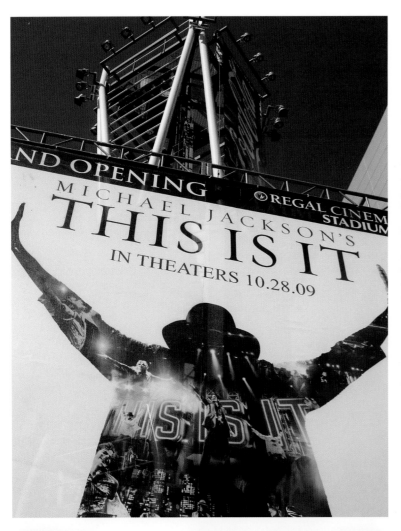

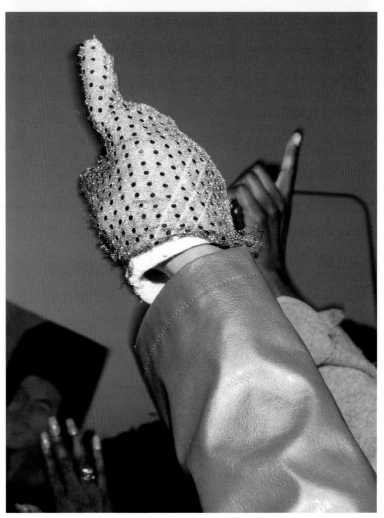

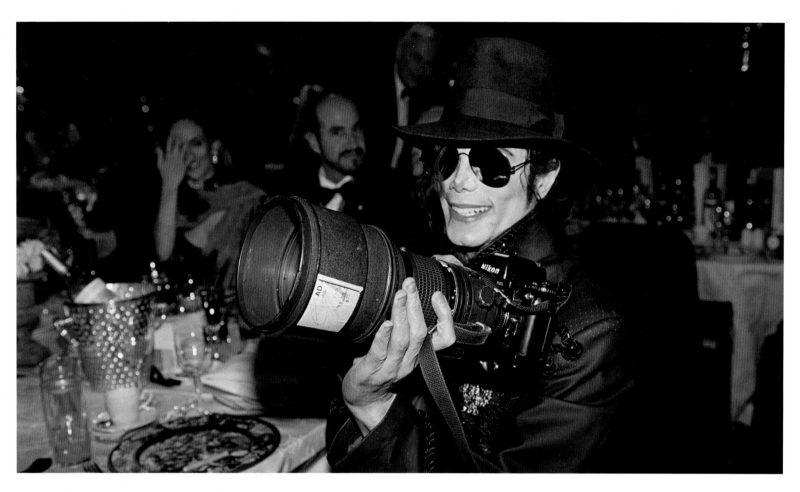

PICTURE CREDITS

ABC/MOTOWN/THE KOBAL COLLECTION – 24 (top), AFP/Getty Images – 37 (top right), 49 (bottom right), 65 (top), 87, 95 (bottom right), 97 (bottom right), 104, 115 (middle), 119 (bottom right), 129 (top right), 133, 146, 149 (bottom left), 155 (top right), 160, ALLEN FREDRICKSON/Reuters/Corbis – (left), Anwar Hussein Collection/Getty Images – 21, AP/Press Association Images – 15, 94, Arlett Vereecke/Rex Features – 49 (top right), Associated Press – 85 (bottom right), Barry Plummer – 25, Berliner Studio Inc./Rex Features – 96 (right), Bettmann/CORBIS – 95 (top), Bill Orchard/Rex Features – 8-9, BuenaVista/Everett/Rex Features – 112 & 112, BuzzFoto/FilmMagic – 120, CBS/Getty Images – 16 (right), 31 (bottom left), Chris Walter/Photofeatures – 78-79, CROLLALANZA/Rex Features – 97 (bottom left), Dana Fineman/Vistalux/Rex Features – 65 (bottom left), 100 (top & middle right), Daniel Morel/Corbis – 157, Duncan Raban/EMPICS Entertainment – 115 (bottom middle), Ed Souza/Pool/Reuters/Corbis – 149 (middle left), Eugene Adebari/Rex Features – 74-75, 76, Everett Collection/Rex Features – 23 (bottom), 34, 40-41, 69 (top right), 72, 110 (bottom), 116 (top), 117, Frank White Agency – 70-71, Gary Gershoff/Retna Ltd/Corbis – 85 (bottom left), Gene Boyars/Star Ledger/Corbis – 114, Getty Images – 31 (bottom right), 36 (top), 38, 49 (top left), 61 (bottom right), 62, 77, 81 (top right), 84, 92 (right) 93 (top right, middle & bottom), 100 (middle left), 102, 107, 111 (right), 113 (bottom right), 115 (top right), 129 (top left), 129 (bottom right), 144 (top right), 144 (bottom), 145 (right), 148, 149 (top left, right & bottom right), 150 (top right), 152, 153, 154, 155 (top left and bottom), 159 (top left), Glenn A Baker/Shooting Star/Idols – pg 56, Harrison Funk/ZUMA Press/Corbis – 7, Herb Ritts/Trunk Archive – 130 & 131, Hulton Archive/Getty Images – 4-5, 30 (bottom), 37 (bottom right), 52 (bottom right), 55 (top left), 65 (bottom right), 96 (left), 105 (top & bottom left), 108, 143 (bottom), 144 (middle right), Joe Bangay/LFI – 127, Joe Giron/Corbis – 100 (bottom), John Issac – 36 (bottom), Jonathan Exley/ContourPhotos.com – 140 & 141, JOSHUA GATES WEISBERG/epa/Corbis – 159 (bottom left and right), Kieran Doherty/Reuters/Corbis – 150 (left), KPA/Zuma/Rex Features – 82, Landov/Retna Pictures – 19 (right), 26, 40 (left), 43, Laura Levine/Corbis – 69 (bottom right), LFI – 17, 30 (top), 31 (middle left), 32, 100 (top right), 111 (left), Lynn Goldsmith/Rex Features – 64 & 69 (top left), Martin Roe/

Retna Ltd./Corbis – 156, Matthew Rolston/Corbis Outline – 151, MCP/Rex Features – 150 (middle), Michael Ochs Archives/Getty Images – 10-11, 14, 16 (left), 18-19, 20 (right), 22 (right), 29 (top & left), 31 (middle right), 42, 44, 48 (top), 55 (bottom right), 57, 61 (bottom left), 61 (top right), 81 (top left), 99 (top left & right), 115 (top left), 139 (left), MPTV/LFI – 128, NBCUPHOTOBANK/Rex Features – 83, Neal Preston/ CORBIS – 22 (left), 33 (bottom), 61 (middle left), 101, 122-123, 125 (left), NEW LINE/THE KOBAL COLLECTION/WRIGHT, K. – 81 (bottom), OPTIMUS PRODUCTIONS/THE KOBAL COLLECTION – 92 (left), PA Archive/Press Association Images – 31 (top), PA WIRE – 109 (bottom left), Redferns/Getty Images – 12-13, 28, 29 right, 31 (centre), 37 (top left), 37 (bottom left), 50, 52 (top), 58, 59, 63, 99 (bottom left & right), 115 (bottom left & right), 134 (top & bottom right), 135, 136, 144 (top left), 144 (middle left), Retna UK – 54 (top), 109 (top), REUTERS/Allen Fredrickson – 31 (bottom middle), Rex Features – 49 (bottom), 97 (top left), RICHARD YOUNG/Rex Features – 86, Robert Mora/ISIPhotos.com/Corbis – 129 (bottom), Ron Galella Collection/WireImage/Getty Images – 45 (bottom right), 105 (bottom right), Roy Garner/Rex Features – 121 (top), SCP/Rex Features – 20 (left), Shaan Kokin/Julien's Auctions/Rex Features – 116 (bottom), SIMON FOWLER/LFI – 51, Sipa Press/Rex Features – 27, 60, 138, 143 (top right), Skyline Features/Rex Features – 90, Sony Music Archive/Getty Images – 145 (left), Sports Illustrated/Getty Images – 129 (middle left), Sportsphoto Ltd./Allstar – 88-89, Stacey Appel private collection – 23 (top) 33 (top left), Steve Schapiro/Corbis – 33 (top left), 35 (left), Steven Paul Whitsitt/ContourPhotos.com – 142, 147, Steven Vaughan/Epic – 91, Sunset Boulevard/Corbis – 110 (top left), Time & Life Pictures/Getty Images – 79, 119 (top and bottom left), 125 (right), Tony Prime – 46 & 47, Unimedia Images/Rex Features – 80 (middle), Universal/Everett/Rex Features – 45 (bottom left), UNIVERSAL/The Kobal Collection – 45 (top), Walter McBride/Retna Ltd./Corbis – 143 (top left), William Snyder/Dallas Morning News/Corbis – 85 (top), WireImage/Getty Images – 6, 49 (bottom left), 52 (bottom left), 55 (bottom left), 66-67, 69 (bottom left), 80 (top), 93 (top left & middle), 97 (top right), 98, 106, 109 (bottom right), 121 (bottom), 127, 139 (left), 158, 159 (top right), ZUMA Press – 60.